NERVOUS READERS BEWARE

I am a sweet and lovely little brother,
innocent of all wrong and doer of only
good deeds . . . Some readers may be
shocked by the appalling physical and
mental torture to which I am subjected
by my big brother and sister on a daily
basis . . .But now I have the power that
comes from being a **REVENGER**

Also available by Jamie Rix published
by Corgi Yearling:

*The War Diaries of Alistair Fury:
Bugs on the Brain*

And for younger readers published
by Young Corgi:

One Hot Penguin

Mr Mumble's Fabulous Flybrows

Other titles by the same author:

Grizzly Tales For Gruesome Kids

Ghostly Tales For Ghastly Kids

Fearsome Tales For Fiendish Kids

More Grizzly Tales For Gruesome Kids

*Johnny Casanova – the unstoppable
sex machine*

The Changing Face of Johnny Casanova

The Fire In Henry Hooter

A Stitch In Time

Free the Whales

The Vile Smile

The Last Chocolate Biscuit

THE WAR DIARIES OF ALISTAIR FURY

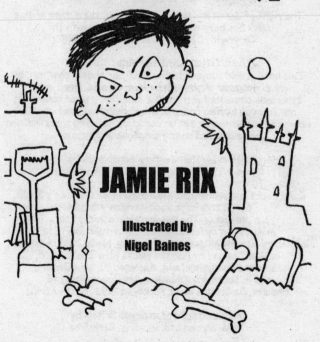

JAMIE RIX

Illustrated by
Nigel Baines

CORGI YEARLING BOOKS

For Max and Harry
who can show this to their friends

THE WAR DIARIES OF ALISTAIR FURY
Book 2: *Dead Dad Dog*
A CORGI YEARLING BOOK : 0 440 865573

First publication in Great Britain

PRINTING HISTORY
Corgi Yearling edition published 2002

3 5 7 9 10 8 6 4 2

Set in 14/16pt Century Schoolbook by
Phoenix Typesetting, Ilkley, West Yorkshire

Corgi Books are published by Random House Children's Books,
61–63 Uxbridge Road, London W5 5SA,
a division of The Random House Group Ltd,
in Australia by Random House Australia (Pty) Ltd,
20 Alfred Street, Milsons Point, Sydney, NSW 2061, Australia,
in New Zealand by Random House New Zealand Ltd,
18 Poland Road, Glenfield, Auckland 10, New Zealand
and in South Africa by Random House (Pty) Ltd,
Endulini, 5a Jubilee Road, Parktown 2193, South Africa

Made and printed in Great Britain by
Cox & Wyman Ltd, Reading, Berkshire.

My Daily Diary

This diary belongs to Alistair Fury

Age 11

Address 47 Atrocity Road, Tooting, England

Country of Birth Slaveland *Nationality* Slavish

Place of Birth That's disgusting! Where does everyone get born from?

Next of kin I have kin that are 'next' in the sense that I clear their hairs out of the sink before I can brush my teeth and they're next in line for the payback treatment, but 'next' in the sense of the people who love me most in the world no matter what . . . I have none. I am as an orphan.

Any distinguishing scars Only mental and they're too deep to see. Except they may show through in my writing, because I'm only human after all. As it says in Shakespeare's Two Merchants of Verona by somebody whose name I forget - 'If you stab me with a compass and twiddle the sharp bit round in the hole, do I not bleed?'

Profession Hit boy

Hobbies Revenge

Notes

'Bring out your dead! Bring out your dead! Come on everyone sling 'em out the

windows!' This is an authentic and true reconstruction of what it must have been like during the plague. Around our house, it is like that again only without the dead bodies, the shouting and the plague. We've got the flu. I have been ill with this fatal lurgy for nearly five days and have missed school all this week. So in case I should die here is my last will and testicle.

The Last Will and Testicle of Alistair Fury

To the Revengers

I leave all my evil thoughts, plus my armoured
go-kart-building diagrams and my plans for
breaking into the zoo and releasing all the
tigers through the sewers so they can pop up
in Miss Bird's class at school and eat her, obviously. I also leave them my brain (which may
not go to medical science, however much mad
scientists might want to harness its *genius*) so
that any brilliant thoughts I might have in the
future can belong to my best friends too.

To my family

I leave my toenails, because they will keep
growing for ever, and one day will be so big that
they will fill the house in every room and there-
fore I will have got a great revenge on my big
brother and sister and my uncaring parents by
making them move out and become homeless.

I am of sound mind.

Alistair Fury

Alistair Fury

My first mistake was getting ill; my second was getting better, because now I am a slave. The rest of my family has caught flu too and is blaming me for giving it to them. Mum and Dad can't work and my big brother and sister, William and Mel, can't go to school. Nor apparently can they get out of bed, make a cup of tea, switch on the radio, scratch their noses or warm the loo seat for themselves! I think I must have got into a time machine and travelled back to Victorian England, because I am nothing more than a scullery maid!

Which is brilliant, because that means my TV-chef mum can't cook, so we can't be poisoned!

It is outrageous. When I complain about my slave duties, I am told to shut up, because it is my fault that everyone's in bed in the first place and I must suffer too.

Which I will do silently, but only so I have a reason to take revenge on my family later!

'So stop being so inconsiderate,' said William. 'If you hadn't got us all so terribly ill, Alice, we'd all be being nice to you.'

He could start by *not* calling me Alice. I AM A BOY! I have conkers in my pocket to prove it.

What's with this 'we're *all* so terribly ill' rubbish? Mum is ill. I can tell that by the way she keeps trying to get up and do stuff, but faints every time she does.

And Dad is ill, because he hasn't been to work at the leisure centre (where as the manager he earns more than a Second Division footballer) for a week. Actually

Dad is more than ill, he's dying! At least that's what he says, and he should know because he reads *Gray's Anatomy* and *The Complete Home Medical Encyclopaedia* all the time.

But William and Mel are having a laugh. Over the last twenty-four hours these are just some of the things I've had to do for my big brother and sister.

'Alistair! Run me a bath. Not too hot and not too cold. And Alistair, don't leave the house in case I need you to pass me a moistened cotton bud to de-wax my ears.'

'Alistair! The radio needs new batteries.'

'Alistair! Change my sheets.'

'Alistair! I need another magazine from the newsagent.'

'Alistair! The video's finished.'

'Alistair! I can't reach my tissues.'

'Alistair!'

'What?'

'Did you put sugar in my tea?'

'Yes.'

'Then it needs more stirring. Would you do it for me?'

Never a please or thank you. Just 'Alistair!' then orders.

And Mel's only staying in bed so she can

10

be well and beautiful again for next weekend when her new boyfriend, Andy, is taking her out for dinner at the Ritz. At least that's what Mel's expecting.

She said to me. 'My new boyfriend's rich. He's got a car.'

'What sort?' I said.

'A Ford Anglia I think.'

'Ooh,' I said. 'Classy.'

'It is, isn't it?' she said.

'Oh yes, it's like a Porsche,' I said.

'A Porsche!' she squealed. 'I knew he was rich!'

'So where's he taking you on this date?' I asked.

'I don't know,' she said. 'It's a secret. Probably the Ritz!'

'Only probably?' I said. 'No way. It's a dead cert!'

Anyway the point is, how ill can Mel be if she can spend two hours a night giggling on the phone to Mr Hot Rod?

I'm exhausted. Home is like a hospital and it is making me ill.

Ha ha! If she believes this she must be iller than I thought – ill in the head!

.FRIDAY.

Feel strong enough to go back to school this morning, but I know that Miss Bird, my scummy form teacher, will only shout at me for being away. Miss Bird is like that. She bears grudges. Me, Aaron and Ralph call her Pigeon because she walks like she's got Nelson's Column stuck up her bottom – all little mincey steps and a great big pecking hooter. Her nose is bigger than a giant eagle's and that's the truth. She also has a temper like a spitting volcano,

MISS BIRD

which means that unless you like being covered in flecks of red-hot gob it's best to either stay on her good side or buy yourself a pair of facial windscreen wipers.

Last time I saw her she thrust my English exercise book under my nose. 'Your handwriting is a scrawl,' she said. 'It looks like an army of blind ants meandering pointlessly across the page. It looks – and

I hope any worms listening will forgive this slur – like a drunken worm with diarrhoea!' To prove her point she then read out a sentence from my last essay in front of the whole class. '*Tar pig war fuss of sandal. In pickled inner up of the cow pit and skunk off in toe the slalom, digging its tall Belinda tit.*'

'That wasn't what I wrote,' I said.

'Oh really?' she replied, with uncalled-for sarcasm.

'Perhaps you'd care to read what you did write then.'

I had a go, but even I found it tricky. '*The dog was full of shame. It picked itself up off the carpet and slunk off into the shadows, dragging its tail behind it.*'

She crossed her arms with a satisfied grunt and called me stupid.

So when Mel and William told me to stay off school for the sake of my health I didn't take much persuading. But at 9.01 a.m., once school registration was done, they stopped being nice to me and treated me like a slave again.

'If you don't answer to our every whim,' said Will, 'we'll tell Miss Bird that you skived off today when you were perfectly healthy.'

'And in future, if you want to quit your job as our nurse,' said Mel, 'you've got to give us at least three months' notice.' If this is a job *why* am I not getting *paid?*

'Because we're family,' said Dad. 'You look after us because you love us. You'd feel awful if you went off to school and never saw me alive again!'

'No I wouldn't,' I said. 'There'd be one less person to cook supper for.' Which made Dad cry. It was a joke! Honestly, sometimes Dad is such an over-emotional girl! Maybe aspirins, nose sprays and secret bottles of beer under the mattress do that to a man!

I have a way with food that makes me think that when I grow up I will be Jamie Oliver.

Cooked lunch for all – frozen peas and rice pudding.

In the middle of cooking, Mum fell into the kitchen. If Mum's fans could have seen her with

Drama Queen

her scarlet face, her hair sticking up like a toothbrush, and her eyes all puffy like a rolled-up pair of rugby socks, they'd never have watched her TV cookery show again. Tried sending her back to bed, but she was away with the fever fairies.

'I'm a mother,' she cried. 'My children need feeding! Soup! That's what we need. Soup!'

15

Then Will joined in, shouting downstairs from his bedroom. 'Calling Nurse Alice! Report to your brother's bedside immediately. The pages of my book need turning.'

apples

Mum passed out on the floor with a ham bone and a stick of celery in her hands. Martyrs like Mum are hard work, but skivers like Will and Mel are evil!

Mrs Muttley, my big-boned piano teacher, just called. Don't know why she bothers to use the phone. Her screechy

voice is so loud I can hear her without it.
She wanted to know why I had missed my
piano lesson yesterday. I told her I was ill.
She said, 'You're never too ill to play piano.'

I said, 'Yesterday, my fingers were
chopped off in a lawnmower accident.'

Blessed silence. I heard her gulp. How
am I going to explain the magical re-growth
of my fingers when I see her next
Thursday?

I need a holiday.

SATURDAY

Full English breakfast in bed ordered by everyone, because it is the weekend. What is a full English breakfast? Found croissant in the freezer and some Bavarian cheese. Sounds pretty English to me. Faces full of disappointment when I delivered it.

Phoned Ralph on his new mobile.

   'Peanut butter and jam sandwiches,' I said. This was our secret club's pass-phrase to let the other person know they were talking to another Revenger.
   Ralph's voice changed immediately. He put on a French accent. 'Speak fellow Revenger,' he said. 'I have peeled back the ears.'

I told him I didn't want to be a home-nurse anymore. 'Easy,' he said. 'The best way to stop someone being ill is to give them nasty medicine.'

'But I haven't got any nasty medicine,' I said. 'And I can't exactly go to a doctor and ask for nasty medicine if all I want it for is revenge.'

'Of course you can,' said Ralph. 'It just depends if he's a real doctor or not!'

Ralph and Aaron came round and helped me work out a cunningly simple plan to pay back my evil brother and sister. I will take

their pictures with a Polaroid camera, then I will tell them that because they are too ill to move I will show the pictures to a doctor for his diagnosis. I'm not going to

really. All I'm going to do is write out a pretend prescription and pass it off as the doctor's, which isn't going to be hard, because every doctor in the world has unreadable handwriting, just like I do! Then I'll pretend to go to a chemist to get the prescription, but instead I'll actually mix up a nasty medicine in the kitchen. And after one huge dose each they won't want another so they'll get better instantly and I'll be released from their slave-master grip!

Phew!

When I took Mel's photo she was sitting up in bed with lumps of pink tissue paper hanging damply from her left nostril. 'I look awful,' she said.

'That's the idea,' I told her. 'So the doctor can see what you really look like.'

'You won't ever show these photos to

anyone else, will you?' she said.

'Never,' I said, thinking, *What a brilliant idea!*

Will was half-asleep with his bum crack showing and a bubble of snot on his tongue. Perfect!

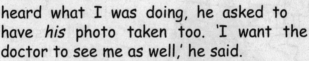

When Dad heard what I was doing, he asked to have *his* photo taken too. 'I want the doctor to see me as well,' he said.

But I wasn't giving nasty medicine to Dad. He could stop my pocket money. 'No. You're too far gone, Dad,' I said. 'You've said yourself that you're going to die, so it's a waste of a film, isn't it? And it's not cheap this Polaroid stuff. About £120 for three photos I think.' Anything to do with spending money usually shuts Dad up. He cried again.

Spent the night forging.

8.00 a.m. – Produced the handwritten prescription and showed it to Mel and William so that they'd think it was real.

'But doctors aren't open on Sunday mornings,' said Will suspiciously. 'So how did you get it?'

'This one is,' I said, thinking as fast as I could. 'He's started a Sunday surgery for people who hurt their knees and get clapping blisters in church.' Not my best lie ever.

'I'll just go and pick it up at the chemist,' I said quickly, running out before they saw me blush.

Pretended to go to the chemist.

All I did really was walk round the block four times till I thought I'd been away long enough. Actually, I *had* to stop walking. I was getting funny looks from a huge man in a balaclava who had locked himself out of his car and was trying to get back in with a metal coat-hanger. He called me a 'nosy little beggar' and threatened to punch me in the bracket if I walked past again. So I didn't.

When I got back I sneaked into the kitchen and made their pretend medicine in the blender, using olive oil, pepper sauce, a whole turnip, anchovy paste, worms and lemon washing-up liquid. It was all going brilliantly, until Mum suddenly lurched into the kitchen to make soup for lunch. I tried to hide my potion by casually lying across the blender, but she asked what I was doing.

'Oh, I'm making soup too,' I said stupidly, to get her off my case.

'What an angel,' she said. 'Bring it up when it's ready.'

What could I do? I'm not a soup chef! I don't know how to make real soup like Mum does. She boils up bones and stuff and makes it the same way as cavemen did hundreds of years ago. She keeps a box of bones in the garden shed. When she wrote her last book *Smells From a Soup Kitchen*, she bought from the butcher every bone that's ever been stripped out of every animal that's ever lived, so she could make soup all day.*

I couldn't even make soup out of a tin, because we don't have any. As a TV chef Mum disapproves of tins. And I only had 7p on me and soup costs more. So what was I to do?

'Alistair!' That was Mum calling again. 'Ready for your soup now!' Mixed up some tomato ketchup with cold water and passed it off as *gestapo*, that cold Spanish soup.

Then after everyone had left it and I had cleared up their trays, I gave Mel and William their revenge medicine!

Actually after all that, it was a rubbish payback, because I was up all night with them being sick into buckets. And when I tried to wash the sick down the bath, little lumps

24

kept sticking in the plughole. I had to use Mum's mascara brush to poke them through.

In between mop-ups, I had a dream. A nightmare really, about my handwriting, in which everything was highly significant.

my highly significant nightmare dream

I am in a supermarket, shopping for my sick family. Me and the lovely Pamela Whitby are shopping together off one long shopping list, like a husband and wife. She is wearing a cardigan and slippers and looks happy, but this can't last, because we're working off a list that's been handwritten by me and neither of us can read it. So I ask a fellow shopper if he can. The man draws a gun and grabs me.

'If I read it right,' he screams, 'this note says you're the only son of an oil billionaire.'

The loveliest girl in the class, but don't tell anyone

'No. It says I need cheese,' I said. 'And loo paper.'

'I am taking you hostage. Nobody try to stop me!'

And I'm kidnapped. My mouth is gagged and I can't speak, so as I'm dragged down the pavement I hand out notes to passers-by which say Help! and Get the Police! but they can't read my writing, so nobody helps. And suddenly I find myself dumped on a desert island by this kidnapper and told that I'll be staying there till the ransom's paid, but I know it never will be. So I chuck bottles into the sea with notes inside begging to be rescued, and the bottles wash up on a beach full of happy tourists, which, as it turns out, is only about fifty yards away across the bay. But of course nobody can read what I've written on my notes. So the happy tourists go on wearing silly hats and rubbing each other's fat red bodies with cooking oil, while I'm stuck on this island for ever.

Weird or what?

Woke up to find my big brother and sister glaring at me in a hurtful manner, because I am going to school and not staying at home to look after them like Indian princes.

'I have to go to school,' I told them. 'If I don't, Pigeon'll give me Saturday morning detentions till the end of my school life!'

'Peanut butter and jam sandwiches,' said Mel, with a cunning smile.

'What do you mean?' I gasped.

'We know what you tried to do to us last night,' she said. 'When I was sick I tasted lemon washing-up liquid.'

That made me feel awful, not to say a little scared that they might tell Mum and Dad I'd tried to poison them, so I made them both tea and toast in bed and ironed William's pyjamas. And that made me late for school.

The class was silent when I walked in.

tumbleweed

Miss Bird fixed me with her beady eyes, like a psychopathic magpie. 'So good of you to join us, Fury. Would it be more convenient if every morning we simply started school twenty minutes later to let you wake up?'

I thought she was being serious. 'Is that possible?' I asked, to which the answer was a low-flying textbook that scraped past my ear. And that was the high spot of the lesson.

very close

Anxious to get a message to Aaron and Ralph I wrote a note on a scrap of paper and passed it along the line. It read: *Meet break. Same place only different. Eat this note when you have read it.*

Unfortunately Aaron was caught with his

mouth full. Pigeon picked the soggy paper off his back teeth, carefully unfolded it and read it aloud. I could see from her ears going red that something was wrong.

'Miss Bird has a huge beaky nose like a pigeon! Don't let the nasty witch read this,' she hissed.

'No!' I shouted. 'That's my bad handwriting again. I didn't write that!' But she didn't want to know what I'd written and I got that detention. After school tomorrow.

Us Revengers can no longer use the Second Year loos for our meetings. The Headmistress banned us after Second Year mothers complained about the extra washing their children kept bringing home during last term's unexplained Damp Trouser Epidemic. So we used the First Year loos for our break time meeting and as usual Ralph stood guard at the door so that no First Years could get in.

I showed my fellow Revengers the photos of Mel and William. We all agreed that my big brother and sister looked so repulsive that these photos would be brilliant weapons for the future.

Then I brought up the problem with the pass-phrase. 'William and Mel have cracked it,' I said. 'Mel winked when she said "peanut butter and jam sandwiches" to me this morning.' Aaron gasped.

'That's a security beach,' he said.

'Is that like a beach where everyone's got a bodyguard?' asked Ralph.

'Something like that,' I said. 'Look, if we were MI5 we'd all have to commit suicide now to protect our secret identities.'

'Would we?' gulped Ralph.

'Yeah, by swallowing exploding pens or sharing a shower with a scorpion, that sort of thing.'

CANAL No 5

Do i really smell that bad?

30

There was only one thing to do. 'Well, I won't do it,' said Ralph. 'I won't kill myself!'

'No. Invent a new code word,' I said. Everyone agreed it was a shame, because *peanut butter and jam sandwiches* was a good one, but we had to do what we had to do, which we did.

Aaron went first. 'How about peanut butter and *jelly* sandwiches?'

'Don't you think we should move away from the peanut butter theme?' said Ralph.

'Keep the jam you mean?'

'Well maybe get rid of the jam, too,' Ralph said. 'Do without any reference to stuff that's spread on toast.'

'OK. How about *marmalade cats like cream*.' That was Aaron again.

'That's fine,' said Ralph, 'but it's still got a jar of spread in it.'

'I know, but that's the clever bit. That's what'll fool 'em, because you can't spread a marmalade cat.'

'Well you can,' I

said, 'but you've got to run it over with a car first.' *Marmalade cats like cream* it was.

Finally we discussed the problem of Aaron's birthday treat on Saturday. His mum said he could take three friends out for a film and a burger chaser. There was me and Ralph and one free space.

'I've invited Pamela Whitby,' he said.

My heart skipped a beat. I have long admired Pamela Whitby. Just the sight of her brings me up in a pash-rash. 'So what's the problem?' I asked brightly.

'You,' he said. 'You've got to come. I'm not asking Pamela if you duck out at the last minute because of nursing duties.'

'I'm coming,' I said. 'No question.' Then. 'By the way did she say anything when she heard I was going to be there?'

'She said "Alistair Who?" And when I told her who, she said to tell you that she doesn't love you, because she still can't remember who you are or what your face looks like, but she doesn't hate you either. Although she said she was sure she *would* if you're anything like every other boy she's ever met.'

I was in heaven. Pamela Whitby had

My Great-Uncle Crawford (Granny Constance's older brother) told me about love once. He said, 'If you can't kiss a girl without standing on a box, find another girl.' Great-Uncle Crawford and me are the same height, so we see things from the same perspective. He's 104 years old, a tiny, shrunken man, who's lived in Ireland all his life. He's so small we call him the leprechaun, and sometimes he can stand at a bar for hours waiting for a drink and the barman doesn't know he's there!

We left the First Year loos with howls of First Year dampness wringing in our ears.

ALICE

Got home to mega mess. Mum had obviously been trying to make soup again. There were bones everywhere. I'm sure out neighbours think we're cannibals, because of the constant smell of boiled bones. I put them back in the garden shed. Then noticed the new shiny copper hood over the hob that had just been fitted to extract Mum's evil cooking smells. The workmen who installed it had dumped a huge pile of bricks and dust on the floor, which had obviously been left for me to clear up. What I need is a witch doctor to wave his magic wand and make my skiving family well again, or better still, a terrifying witch to scare them all out of bed! *Eureka!*

Have just looked up *witch* in Yellow Pages. It said *See under Covens*, but there was nothing there either. Except for one advert:

Bill Nash

Electrical Engineer.

All kitchen appliances repaired.

I think Bill Nash has been misfiled.

TUESDAY

Had a brilliant idea at school. Aaron said, 'Haven't you got a granny who's a monster? The one who shaves and carries an electric cattle prod in her handbag in case a refugee asks her for money?'

'Granny Constance!' I said.

'That's her,' said Aaron. 'She's a sort of witch. Why don't you go round and ask her tonight?'

'Don't be stupid,' I said. 'How will I get out of the house without William and Mel suspecting something's up?'

'Take Mr E for a walk,' he said.

'What!' I said. 'Take Mr E for a walk! What planet are you from, Aaron? Nobody takes Mr E for a walk! He's a pug dog with a hideous beige-coloured face that looks like someone's kicked it flat with a boot. He's so disgustingly ugly it's embarrassing to be seen on the streets with him!'

I think they'd be doing the human race a big favour if they took the insides out of every pug dog and turned them into hand-warmers like those furry muffs that Russian women wear on sleighs. And another thing that makes Mr E embarrassing to take out,* is that last time Mum did it, he stopped in front of a long bus

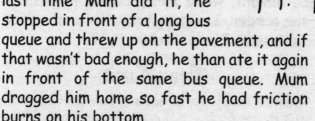

queue and threw up on the pavement, and if that wasn't bad enough, he than ate it again in front of the same bus queue. Mum dragged him home so fast he had friction burns on his bottom.

Spent rest of day at school trying to think of a better excuse for leaving the house than taking Mr E for a walk. Was so busy thinking I nearly forgot Miss Bird's detention. I had to write out one hundred times: *I must not write rude notes about my pretty teacher with the small button nose.* But because she can't read my handwriting I wrote: *I must tell the world that my ugly teacher has a nose like a pigeon,* and she never noticed! A small victory, but a victory nonetheless.

Got home and went round to see the witch. She wasn't in so I left a note. I took Mr E with me, but wore a big peaked cap to cover my face and Mel's coat so everyone would think I was Mel if they saw me with the ugly pug. Actually, Mr E was perfectly behaved on our walk, wasn't sick once and even carried a small leaf home in his mouth, which was *nearly* sweet.

Tonight, while Mr E buried his leaf in the garden, I said my prayers for the first time since I was a baby.

Dear Lord

I don't usually pray, not unless I want something, and tonight I do want something. Nothing selfish, just a whopping great favour for me. Make Pamela Whitby like me. Actually I'll be honest, just 'not hating' me would be a good start. Make Pamela Whitby 'not hate' me enough to smile in my direction, even if it's a smile meant for someone behind me and I'm just sort of vaguely in the way, like a bodyguard taking a bullet for the President. Thank you Lord.

May the force be with you.

Amen etc etc etc.

Actually no. I bet the bombs took one look at her and were so scared they went back home!

6.45 a.m. – The revenge-witch arrived! Dad's monster mum, Granny Constance, strode into the hall and slammed the door behind her. She must have had a hard life, because she looks like she disapproves of everything. Maybe she had lots of near misses by bombs in the war.

She threw off her coat and rolled up her sleeves. She was already wearing an apron underneath, and when I tried to kiss her she handed me her hat.

'Where is everyone?' she said in her clipped Irish accent. 'It's nearly seven o'clock, Alistair. Nobody ever grasped the day by rising after six thirty! Is this from you?' She smoothed out the note I'd written the night before.

'*Granary heap!* she read. '*Grinny, serve us pies. Wheel too seek and wick to log-a feet our shelves. Loo yob fat-floor-mite gruntzone, Apestir.* It must be from you. I recognize the abysmal handwriting. What does it mean?'

'It means,' I said, '*Granny, help! Granny save us please. We're all to sick and weak to look after ourselves. Love your favourite grandson, Alistair.*' She agreed to stay for one day, long enough to sort out my lazy family once and for all. Ha ha!

Went to school, but not before my personal hand *Gran*-ade had gone off with a bang.

Get it?

40

The effect she had was brilliant. She turned off tellies, opened draughty windows, cooked up semolina, force-fed castor oil, set boring puzzles and vacuumed so loudly that nobody could sleep. As I was leaving I heard her shouting up the stairs; 'Dormitory inspection at nine. I want hospital corners on all of your beds and God help you if I find one stray hair on a pillow. Lunch is *downstairs* at twelve – rollmop herrings and crispbread.'

Mel and William arrived at school at 11.45, just before lunch, having made a remarkably quick recovery from the flu.

It was lucky they hadn't arrived earlier, otherwise they'd have seen us Revengers pinning up their pictures. As it was, half the school was already laughing at them. Aaron, Ralph and I watched from behind a pillar as the crowd parted and William and Mel walked slowly towards the board

41

where their instant *photo-larphs* were on display. Under Mel's picture we'd written: *Hi. Think I'm sexy? Then give me a call at the Dog's Home. That's 0600 655 77 856*

And we'd put William's photo under a big caption saying: WANTED: *Handsome princess to save this Sleeping Beauty! Wake me with a kiss!*

William was fighting off all the boys' kissing lips when he heard Ralph, Aaron and me snort. He and Mel gave chase. I could hear them catching up, so to make them think I was innocent, I screamed, 'It was an *accident*!'

I was hoping they'd believe me and stop, but William was already gripping the back of my collar. Luckily, that was when the five of us ran into Miss Bird, knocking her books across the corridor.

Outside the detention room, William and Mel grabbed me by the throat, pinned me up against the wall and asked if I would like to do their lines for them. Naturally, being a loving brother I said, 'Get lost, pig bums!' which I then quickly changed to 'Yes certainly, you two lovely people,' when Mel tweaked my nipples till they hurt.

But I knew that Miss Bird knew my handwriting. When we all handed our lines in, she recognized it on William and Mel's papers, as I knew she would! I was allowed to go home, while they had to sit there for another hour until they'd done their lines themselves. And fifty *extra* ones too!

When I got home Mum had recovered too. Enough to drive Granny Constance home. Apparently the older interferer had been binning Mum's precious soup bones, shouting, 'And this one's past its smell-by date too!'

Dad was crying. Mum has told him he's got a disease that hasn't been discovered yet. She looked up his symptoms in his medical encyclopaedia – always tired, addicted to rubbish TV shows, dependent on others for all his needs, an increased consumption of beer, and spilling large quantities of Tex Mex food down his pyjamas – and there was nothing listed.

AN EVENING WITH DRAMA QUEEN DAD

'Do you think that means I'm going to die?' he asked me.

'I hope not,' I said. More tears. Then he gave me twenty quid and told me to run down the shops and buy him a will.

'You can help me fill it in,' he said. 'It'll be good handwriting practice for you. And hurry, Alistair, or I might not be here when you get back!'

On the way to the newsagent I composed a poem on Dad dying.

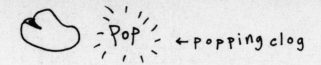

POP ← popping clog

Finally I have something to say
Dad, please do not die today.
If you go and pop your clogs
Who will pay my pocket mon-ay?

Composing Dad's will was horrible. His illness has made him tired and over-emotional and he said stuff about our family that I don't need to know. Like how often he kisses Mum.

Yuck!

How gloss is that?

To my darling wife, Miss Kiss Funny-dumpling, whose lips have shared a million puckering passions, who tickled my toes when I was ill and soothed my brow with a Wet Wipe. I leave love, memories, a house and a bank account

I'm eleven years old. I don't want to know that someone calls my mum *Miss Kissy Funny-dumpling*. She's MY mum. She makes soup, washes clothes, shouts a lot, makes my life a misery and smells nice. That's enough.

'To my first child, Melanie, beautiful, talented Melanie. If you love your old dad half as much as he loves you, never cut your hair. Remember his pearls of wisdom on how to deal with men and you'll never go wrong in the love department: Once bitten . . . twice shy. Twice bitten . . . put a muzzle on him and chain him up in the garden.

I leave you lots of money. Ask your mum.

To my brave, clever, eldest son, William, Adonis, Apollo and a quality scrum-half too. I shall always remember your first smile that you did just for me and not for your mum as she always claimed. Ours was a special bond, William. Deep and unspoken. Father to son. Man to man. I leave you my car, my AA membership . . .

I stopped Dad in the middle of writing this down. 'This is a will, Dad, not a book. You've just got to state facts.'

'I thought I was,' he said all hurt like a baby. 'Right. *To my youngest son, Alistair. Goodbye*

46

and thanks for all the Christmas presents that I forgot to thank you for when I was alive. Here's a fiver.'
Then he stopped. I waited for more.

'Is that it?' I said.

'You told me to keep it short.'

'Yeah, but you said loads of stuff about everyone else that sounded like you loved them, but you made me sound like someone you'd just met on a bus.' Now it was my turn to feel hurt and upset. I didn't care how ill my dad was he didn't deserve me. 'To my father,' I said, 'I leave you this pen so you can sign your stupid will yourself!' Then I left the room and locked myself into my bedroom, because William and Mel had just stormed in from their double detention and I did not want to be flower-pressed in the ironing board again!

During supper, I stuck close to Mum for protection. It meant I had to help her with the washing-up, but I didn't care. William splashed me with soup, and he and Mel pretended I was invisible until I spoke these words, 'Can I have some new clothes for Saturday, Mum?' I hated having to ask. If I had an allowance like the other two I could buy *what* I wanted *when* I wanted it. As it is, Mum still buys my clothes, which

47

means that my clothes are pants whereas theirs are quality.

'What do you want new clothes for Saturday for?' asked Mel.

'Have you got a little girlfriend?' taunted William. 'Do you want new clothes to make her think you're good-looking and kiss you?'

'It's Aaron's birthday,' I said.

'Oh it's a *boyfriend*,' shrieked William. 'Alice has got a boyfriend, Mummy.'

'Lovely, darling.'

Why do mums never listen to anything we say? The only time my mum ever hears me is when I say something I don't want her to hear. Like, 'How was I to know cats got sick in tumble driers?'

'But I haven't got a boyfriend!' I shouted. 'It's not true!'

And that was when William and Mel pretended I was speaking a foreign language. 'No, sorry, Alice, can't make head nor tail of what you're saying. No comprendo. It's all gibberish.'

'I know,' said Mel, 'why don't you write down what you want to say about your boyfriend.'

'I haven't got a boyfriend!' I yelled.

'Write it down,' said William, 'or we can't

understand.'

So I wrote it down, but it didn't make any difference, because they just pretended they couldn't read my handwriting.

'*I love my boyfriend,*' read William falteringly. 'Is that what this says?'

'No!' I screamed. '**I DON'T HAVE A BOYFRIEND!**' It was no good. Mel and William had got their teeth into me and weren't letting go. So I let them have it. 'One day Dad's going to die,' I said, 'and then I'll have my own money and then I'll be able to buy what I want, and what I want *won't* be *you!*' And when I looked round, Mum and Mel were crying.

'You callous brute!' shouted William. 'You've upset them now by saying Dad's going to die!'

'Dad!' bellowed Mel. 'Alice wants you to die!'

'No I don't!' I said.

'He's going to kill you!' hollered William.

I went to bed. I am never mentioning shopping again. It is a subject that inflames passions – like crutch rot.

Good night, Pamela.

Had another dream last night.

Last Night's Dream

Pamela and I are shopping in Knightsbridge. I've got a huge gold credit card with enough money on it to buy a boat. We're like a Playboy couple because we're both wearing dark glasses and wearing flash clothes. She's got a scarf over her expensive hair cut and I'm wearing a suit with silver buttons. And we're driving along in a red Ferrari with the roof down and she's got Mr E on her lap like one of those little dogs that really rich people have. And Mr E's been sick on her lap, but she doesn't care because she can buy another dress and anyway he's eating it up again. And we're stopping at all the flash clothes shops – CK, Hugo Boss, Armani, Man at Argos – and I go in and buy what I like and come out with tons of boxes. It's brilliant. And we turn to each other on the pavement and I say, 'Life's so much better since Dad died. We've got all the money in the world.' And we both nod at the truth, but there's one thing I'm not happy with. Everyone's suddenly pointing at me. Policemen appear from side streets and run towards me. I

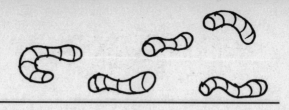

try to run away, but there's a weight on my shoulders dragging me down, and when I look back I see what I'm towing behind me – it's a lump of writhing maggots! It's Dad's dead body!

Woke in a sweat. This was William and Mel's fault for putting Dad's ghost in my head. Little niggles and jibes I can take, but messing with my head deserves payback. So, nicked Dad's will from his bedside table and changed it by crossing out what Dad had told me to write and putting in what I thought was better.

To Mel and William I leave diddly-squat, because they're a horrid ~~brother and sis~~ children who deserve to get a good kicking.

To my favourite child, Alistair, I leave everything (except what Mum needs to live a comfortable life in an Old Folk's Home).

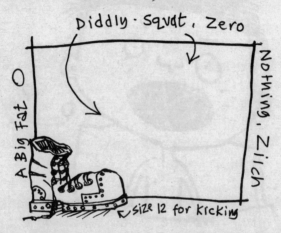

The clever bit of my plan was that it was my handwriting I was changing so the changes didn't look like changes. Well, they *did* look like changes, but changes made by the person who wrote the will in the first place, which everyone will assume was Dad. The other clever bit was remembering all the time that it was Dad writing the words not me. I spotted 'brother and sis . . .' so I can't be stupid!

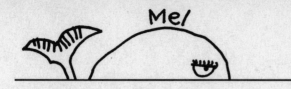

Took the will down to breakfast, where Mum was sitting with a towel over her head and her head over a large bowl of soup that she was sucking up through her nostril.

'Why don't you use a spoon?' I asked.

'Id's ad idhalation,' she said. 'Clears de tubes.'

Mel and William walked in. This was my moment. 'Look what I found upstairs,' I said cunningly. 'Dad's will. Sit down. It's going to come as a terrible shock. I'm so sorry, I thought Dad loved us all the same.' Their faces were a picture! They didn't know what they were going to hear next. 'Read it for yourselves,' I said, trying not to snigger.

If I was to take up acting as a profession, I honestly think some people would ask me to stop, because I'm so good that other actors would never get any work – except for Carol Boring-woman, Pauline Squirt, Caroline Biscuit-tin, and Trevor Macdonut who have to be in everything that's ever on TV these days. And anyway, I wouldn't be going up for their parts, would I? I'm *not* a newsreader, I'm *not* a woman and I'm *not* fat.

Mel and William couldn't read my handwriting so I had to read it to them. They listened to their fate in silence. I swear the blood drained right out of them, because when they looked up they were both as white as sheets.

'Oh dear,' said William.

'It's really tragic, isn't it?' I smirked.

'It's not funny, Alice. You're in real trouble.' This was not what I was expecting to hear. 'If Dad was to die now and you were to inherit all his money, what would the police think?'

'Murder?' suggested Mel.

'Yes,' said William. 'Youngest son gets nothing in the original will so changes it in his favour. Then bumps the old man off.'

'But I didn't,' I said. 'I mean I haven't. I won't.'

'His only mistake,' smiled Mel, 'was not disguising his very distinctive handwriting.'

'But Dad told me to do it!' I said panicking.

'But how can that be, Alice?' said William

pointing to my crossing out. 'Because we're not dad's brother and sis . . . are we? Do they still hang people for murder these days, Mel?'

'No, William, they just bang them up in a Bad Boy's Prison with axe-murderers and child-eaters. Let's hope Dad gets better, Alice, for your sake, because if he dies . . .' My big brother and sister snorted with laughter.

Suddenly felt stupid and wished I hadn't been so hasty. I didn't know it was illegal to

change a will.

'It was an *accident*,' I shouted. 'I spilled coffee over the will and it washed away the ink, all the letters and words and things, so I tried to remember what the words were and write them back in so no-one would notice, but I must have got them wrong.' Even I wasn't convinced by my story. Nor was William.

'Dead man walking,' he said. 'Dead man walking!'

I could hear my heart beating.*

I felt sick. Not even when Mum said from under the towel, 'Alistair, I *will* take you shopping. After school today. It's just what we need to put us back on our feet after this nasty flu,' could I be shaken from my fear. All I could hear in my head was the rattle and clang of a prison door!

At school, Ralph and Aaron were cross.

'You've only got yourself to blame,' said

Ralph. 'The Revengers are a team. We act *together* or not at all. You cough, I cough. He coughs, we all cough.'

'Why?' said Aaron. 'What's wrong with my cough? Why does everyone get infected by my cough and not by yours?'

'It's like the Musketeers,' said Ralph. 'Strength in numbers. I scratch your back, you scratch mine. He scratches my back, we all scratch each others' backs.'

'Now I've got fleas!' said Aaron. 'Are you saying I don't bath, Ralph?'

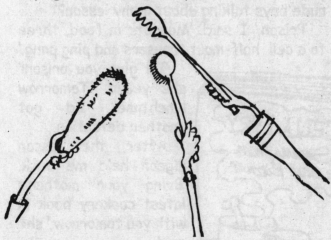

'No, I'm saying have patience. Alistair should have brought his plan to us first. We could have told him that changing a will often leads to beheaditation.'

'It was an *accident*,' I said. This was my story and I was sticking to it.

'QUIET!'

The pigeon was trying to explain what Chaucer meant by 'throng'. 'What are you rude boys talking about in my lesson?'

'Prison,' I said. 'Maggots in food, three to a cell, half-mast trousers and ping pong.'

'I'll give you prison!' she yelled. 'Tomorrow lunchtime!' I'd got another detention.

After the lesson Pigeon held me back. 'Bring your mother's latest cookery book in with you tomorrow,' she said.

'*Smells From a Soup Kitchen?*' I asked.

'That's it,' she said.

'Ridiculously priced at £25.'

I said I would when really I just wanted to know why.

At lunch, used Ralph's phone to call Dad and check he wasn't dying, but there was no reply. Had visions of him lying on the floor unable to reach the phone. Kept thinking, if he had one of those distress flares around his neck like they give to old people and round-the-world yachtsmen, he could fire red smoke into the sky and I could run back and save his life.

On the way home, tried to buy him

By Jove Smithers, they're sending flares up

flares, but bizarrely the shop in which I'd seen them advertised only sold trousers.

Bought him a box of cheap chocolates instead, because that's what everyone gets in hospital to make them better.

When I got home I was greeted by Mel and William. They were standing in the hallway with long sad faces. They both kissed me and ruffled my hair and tried to force kindly smiles.

'Where's Dad?' I said nervously.

Mel looked like she was going to cry. 'He's gone . . .' she choked and couldn't finish.

'He's gone!' I shouted. 'But he can't go. It's not my fault.' I started running up the stairs, only to hear Mel finish her sentence behind me.

'He's gone . . . to the loo!' she laughed.

I banged on the door. 'Dad, are you in there?'

60

'If you're after *Golf Monthly*, you'll just have to wait,' he said.

'So you're not nearly dead?' I said. 'I've bought you stuff to make you all right again.'

'Just as well,' he said. 'I can't seem to beat this disease.'

When he came out of the loo I helped him back to bed and told him I loved him and would never do anything to harm him, and to prove it I gave him his mobile phone to keep next to him so that if ever he felt like he was dying he could call me for help.

'When did you get a mobile phone?' he said.

'What?' I said. 'I haven't got a mobile phone.'

'So how can I call you then?' I hate technology. If you're not at the cutting edge it makes you feel so inadequate. Just then Mum called. Time for shopping. In all the panic I'd forgotten.

In the hall, before we got in the car, I also told Mum that I loved Dad, so that if the police asked her if I was a murderer she'd say no.

'What is wrong with him?' I asked. 'Everyone else seems to be getting better. He's just getting worse.'

'And will do for the next two weeks,' she said.

I was horrified. 'Why? What's he got? You know something, and you're not telling us!'

'He's got two weeks of safety inspections at work,' said Mum, 'which is more hassle than he knows what to do with.'

Now I'm confused. Does that mean Dad's really ill or not ill at all?

Forgot all about Dad when I got in the car and saw Mel and William sitting in the back seat.

'What are *they* doing here?' I said to Mum. 'I thought this was a special trip – just you and me. We never spend quality time together.'

'Oh don't be ridiculous, Alistair. They asked me to come. William's got to buy something for the rugby club lunch and Mel's got a date.'

'But they've got an allowance. They can spend their money when they want to. They only want to spend it now to wreck my trip.'

'I'm not listening,' said Mum. 'This is stupid.'

I bet if she'd looked in her mirror she'd have seen them sniggering. I pulled the lever under the seat and shot backwards

62

over William's shins.

'Ow!' he squealed.

'Sorry,' I said innocently. 'It was an *accident!*'

We drove to the shops in silence. Mum's mobile phone rang and I answered it. It was Dad checking that Mum's mobile phone was working so he could call if he needed anything.

I knew this shopping trip was going to be a disaster. I wanted to go into streetwise shops like Pin, Pukka, Pie, Rap, Rip, Tide, and Tag where all the shop assistants were young and rude, but Mum chose Thomas Brothers Department Store – *Quality Clothes at a Price that's Nice!*

'Because there's room for growth in their clothes, Alistair.'

'There's room for a wheelchair,' I muttered. 'They're for old people.'

We spent the first hour looking at black dresses for Mel. The first one she tried on looked fine and we all told her so, but she wasn't sure if it made her look fat. Mum said it didn't, but Mel is a girl and still had to try on every other black dress that had ever been made in the world, and then, just when I was hoping for a meteorite to smash up her changing room, she tried on the first one again!

'This'll do fine,' she said. I narrowed my eyes and pointed to my watch.

Next of course was William. Second oldest always goes second, which condemned me* to bottom spot. William needed something smart to pass him off as 18 in the rugby club bar. I suggested a balaclava, but nobody laughed. It took another three-quarters of an hour to decide which pair of 'stay-pressed' slacks made him look tallest and which button-down shirt made him look oldest. He chose well. In his comfortable new clothes he looks like Great Uncle Crawford's twin.

It was 5.20 when mum asked me what I wanted. The store closed in ten minutes.

'I don't know,' I said, which drew a weary chorus of 'Oh come on Alice' from my brother and sister. 'We haven't got all day to hang around here waiting for you to make up your mind.'

'All right,' I said. 'Trousers. Sexy trousers and a T-shirt with WOW on the back or something funny like that.'

Mel shivered and covered her face with her hands. 'This is so embarrassing,' she muttered.

'Go away,' I said.

'How about these?' said Mum, picking up the nearest pair of trousers she could find. They were yellow.

'No,' I said.

'Oh come on, Alistair!' she sighed. 'There

65

isn't time to be fussy! If I've made the effort to bring you here, the least you can do is try them on!'

It felt like I'd been put on a train I didn't want to be on, and it was leaving the station before I could get off. I took the trousers and turned to go into the changing room.

'No, here,' Mum said. 'There's nobody around. It'll be quicker.'

'What?' She wanted me to drop my trousers in the middle of Thomas Brothers Department Store! Had she gone mad?

So there I was, scarlet with embarrassment, Mel and William giggling, no trousers on and about a million shoppers staring at my down-belows, when a man with a camera approaches Mum and says he's from the local paper. 'Celia Fury? TV chef? Harold Hodges from the *Tooting Tribune*. Can I get a picture for our gossip page – *The Stars Are Out in Tooting*. Do you mind? You and your lovely family?'

And before I know what's happening, Mum's all celebrity-smile, William and Mel are cosying up for a group hug and I'm standing in the middle in my underpants!

'I don't want my photo taken like this!' I said.

'Smile, little girl,' said the photographer.

'I'm a BOY!' I said. 'I'll show you my conkers.'

'If you don't want the photo taken,'

And I was standing there in my underpants! How many more clues did he want?

67

William whispered in my ear, 'Spoil it. Stick your finger through the front of your pants, then when they develop it they'll think it's obscene and chuck it away.'

'Do you think it'll work?'

'Of course.'

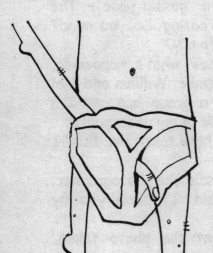

'Thanks,' I said, sticking my finger through the Y of my Y-fronts. I had misjudged William. Sometimes he could be really nice and a pleasure to be related to.

Anyway the photo was taken and then it was 5.30. I explained to Mum that I hated the yellow trousers because a) they were yellow, b) they were yellow and c) they were yellow, but she said it was them or nothing, and she hadn't come all this way just to waste her time, so yellow trousers it was. I shall never wear them, nor the matching yellow shirt she

68

snatched off a shelf by the check-out. How can I face Pamela Whitby looking like a canary?

As we were leaving Mum's phone rang again. I answered it.

'Hello Alistair,' said Dad in a weedy voice. 'I'm still ill, so don't go telling your Mum I'm not. Thing is, normally I've just got the appetite of a little baby sparrow, but right now I could do some serious damage to a Chinese take-away and a nice bottle of cold rice wine. OK?'

I told Mum.

Outside, William and Mel burst into another fit of laughter.

'What have I done this time?' I said.

'I can't believe you actually did it!' hooted William. 'Sticking your finger through your pants! Of course they're going to publish that photo now. It's a

scoop! *Celia Fury in Sex-Mad Shopping
Orgy!* The police are bound to get involved.
They'll have to – it's a public indecency
what you've done, Alice!'

'If it's not murder it's flashing!' said Mel.
'Do you *want* to go to prison, little
brother?'

I am a depressed fugitive. And I'm never
going shopping with Mum ever again. I
volunteered to fetch Dad's take-away just
to get away from my stupid family.

Disaster! Dad has got food poisoning from
the Chinese food. We were downstairs
when he rang us up from the loo to say he

was being sick. Now William and Mel are talking about the police again in hushed voices.

'It's obvious what they're going to think,' said Mel.

'After all, you were the one who got the take-away.'

'I just fetched it,' I said. 'I didn't cook it.' But that was irrelevant apparently, because there was still plenty of time between picking the food up at the counter and getting back in the car for me to have slipped the poison in!

Wish the phone would stop ringing! First, thought it was the police, but it was just Andy for Mel. Second time, thought it might be the prison wanting to measure me up for my prison clothes, but it was Andy again. Third time, thought it might be the undertakers wanting my size for the coffin they were going to build for when I was

71

hanged! I might have guessed it was Andy.

4.00 a.m. I have just woken from another bad dream.

Another Bad Dream

I'm in prison wearing yellow prison fatigues and the only visitor I get is Pamela Whitby. She's baked me a cake and as she leaves she winks and says there's something in the cake that I might like. Then I'm back in the cell, tearing the cake apart looking for a metal file to saw through my bars and all I can find is a small bottle of blue dye and a note: If you don't change the colour of your clothes I shall stop loving you.

FRIDAY

Knew it was going to be a bad day when I got out of bed and stepped on Napoleon, our cat. He screeched and sprang from the floor onto the window ledge. Only on account of him having no tail, he lost his balance, fell out of the window, rolled down the roof and flipped over the guttering into the garden. I thought cats were always supposed to land on their feet. So why did Napoleon land on his head in a watering can?

On way to the bathroom Mel did oh-so-funny *neenaw-neenaw* siren noises in my ear. Then she said, 'I haven't got enough space to hang up my new black dress, so I thought I'd borrow your wardrobe, OK?'

No please or thank you. She just barged into my bedroom and when I came out of the bathroom all my

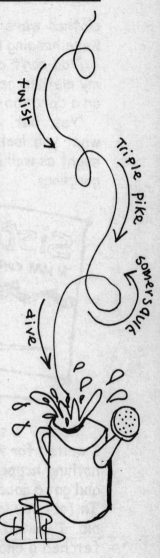

73

clothes were in a heap, while all of hers were hanging neatly in my cupboard.

'You can't do that!' I said. 'What about *my* clothes getting creased? I'm going out on a date too you know.'

'Yes, but you're a boy. Nobody cares what you look like,' said Mel. 'Whereas I might as well commit suicide if I don't look gorgeous.'

'Really?' I said. 'You don't look gorgeous.' I waited for Mel to honour her words, but nothing happened, so I popped downstairs and got a good strong rope from the cellar. 'In fact you look hideous. Really puffy and old.' I waited again. Again no suicide, so I fetched a chopper from the kitchen. 'Well go on then, dog-face. Top yourself.'

Mel put the chopper on a table and stormed off. I knew her offer was too good to be true!

Just as I was leaving for school, the phone rang. It was Mrs Muttley asking why I'd missed my piano lesson again.

'I would have phoned,' I said, 'but without fingers I can't press the buttons to dial. Or pick up the phone in fact.'

'So how did you answer the phone just now?' she screeched.

'With my tongue,' I said.

'Then how can you speak?' she said. 'If you're holding the phone in your tongue?'

'My tongue's double jointed!'

'Are you lying to me?' she said.

'No,' I said. 'It's true.' She said if I was not there next week she'd take it as a personal insult. Must remember not to be there next week.

75

No sooner had I put the receiver down than it rung again. This time it was Dad phoning down on his mobile to see if everyone had forgotten him.

'No,' I said. 'You never forget who your dad is.'

'I meant has everyone forgotten I'm ill.'

'You sound better,' I said hopefully.

'I'm not,' he said. 'But at least that Chinese food's all out now.' I asked him how he knew. 'Water chestnuts float,' he said. 'I counted them all in and I counted them all out again.'

'So you're not going to die?' I checked.

'Only of hunger,' he replied. I made him breakfast in bed.

They do say that when you've been in bed as long as Dad has, you forget how to live with normal human beings and develop a fear of the outside world. If I was his doctor, I'd prescribe something to make him get up – like a house fire.

At school I was desperate to meet the Revengers to plan some revenge, but we couldn't get together till lunchtime and even then we had to do Pigeon's detention first. While the others did lines, she pulled me aside and asked if I'd brought my mum's new cookery book. I showed it to her.

'Good,' she said. 'I want you to start at the beginning and copy out every recipe exactly, in your neatest handwriting. And if you don't finish today, you can carry on in your next detention.'

'What next detention?' I said. 'I may never get another one in my life.'

'Oh, you will,' she said. 'Trust me.'

'Do you want me to copy out the bit on the back cover about Mum?' I said.

'No, no, no,' she snapped. 'Just the recipes. I can't cook *the bit on the back cover about Mum*, can I?'

'She just wants your mum's book free,' whispered Aaron when I sat down.

'Easy peasy revenge though,' said Ralph. 'Copy out the recipes *wrong*! Add a few nasties – chillies, and extra tablespoon of pepper, some octopus ink! She won't know whether she's coming or going.'

'She'll be going,' I sniggered, 'every five minutes!'

The bell rang for afternoon lessons before I could sort out revenges for William and Mel. We ran down the corridor towards Pigeon's classroom, but halfway there I stopped and sauntered.

'What are you doing?' shouted Ralph. 'Hurry up, or you'll get another detention.'

'I know,' I said. Ralph's revenge idea was too good to miss! Successfully secured my fourth detention in four days.*

Adjusted Mum's much-loved recipes, as follows:

1) To the broth of steaming scallops, prawns and clams with black beans, coriander and lime, I added a handful of stinging nettles and two large chicken's feet.

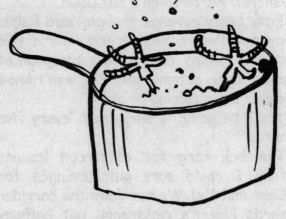

2) To a vegetarian soup of mung beans and fresh herbs, I added some left-over pork fat.

3) In the recipe for sweet peppers and celeriac soup, I added that old gardener's favourite - nine tablespoons of finely diced leaves.

4) And finally I gave a lift to the soup Mum had called stuffed, rolled and baked sardines with pine nuts and fresh herb soup, by adding chopped mouse to the stuffing.

Then I handed the bits of paper in to Miss Bird, pointed out that she was salivating from the corners of her mouth, and went home hoping that she was cooking tonight!

Good news, I think. Dad still can't get out of bed or cook for himself, obviously, but feels strong enough to tackle a large gin and tonic. The alcohol kills the germs apparently.

Mel has decided that she needs forty-eight hours to get ready for her Sunday date with Andy. This means she's trying on every piece of clothing she owns seven times. As all her clothes are in my bedroom, I am banished to the sitting room all night and forced to sit with a mum who thinks me ungrateful and doesn't like me. Tried tickling her toes to break the tension, but it turns out she hates that too, especially when I poke a hole in her sock.

Tried to go to bed early, but couldn't get into my room. Mel has left it in such a mess that the door won't open. Behind it is a clothes mountain. My bed is buried. I can't sleep there. When I protested to Mel she locked herself in the bathroom to stick on those long false nails that make girls look like Edward Scissorhands, and pretended she couldn't hear.

Went back downstairs and <u>slept on the</u> sofa. When I told Mum why, she said, 'Fine, I was just going to bed anyway. No sitting up late though, and no watching any naughty films.'

So that is how it is. If I am to make my own way in this big bad world I'm on my

own. No-one will fight my battles for me. I have to find my own inner warrior. As they say on the telly in that famous action adventure kung-fu thriller film set in the Arctic, 'I am going now to seek my Ninja Turtle. I may be some time.'

To pay back Mum for her inconsideration I did sit up and watch a naughty film – *The Phantom of the Opera*. It was the most terrifying thing I have ever seen. I had hairs sticking up on the back of my neck, goosebumps, sweaty armpits, the works! When Mr E nudged open the sitting room door and Napoleon leapt onto my shoulders like a huge hairy hand, I actually screamed and jumped off the sofa. Lasted ten minutes before I switched the whole thing off. Why does anyone watch scary movies? They're *scary*.

me

11.30 p.m. – I am completely awake and think I might be mad. Outside our house there is ghostly piano music playing. I can hear a spooky piano tinkling through the wall. This is like what happened in the *Phantom* film. If I am shortly to become a grisly victim of the loopy piano-playing madman in the sewers, I really hope he doesn't kill me to the tune of *Super Trouper* by Abba, because that is Mrs Muttley's favourite tune and I'd hate to die thinking of her!

Now that I'm awake, I cannot believe that I have got through a whole day without thinking up good revenges on Mum, William and Mel, especially after what they have done to destroy my life! I phoned Ralph's mobile to pick his brains for evil ideas. But when the phone was answered, it wasn't Ralph. I know, because I said, 'Marmalade cats like cream,' and a gruff voice said, 'Tooting Police, can I help you?'

Brain picking!

I slammed the phone down in a panic. How had that happened? I might have misdialled, but what if I'd pressed redial by mistake? What if someone else had been phoning the police earlier? What if Dad was dead and I was about to be arrested?

Ran upstairs to check on Dad. He wasn't dead. He was snoring like an elephant seal and Mum was sleeping next to him with a tissue in either ear. She looked like she had one long tissue pulled right through her head.

So why had I called the police? Was it a mistake or was it guilt? Was I ready to confess or was I somehow inside an episode of the *X Files*? And why was the piano outside now playing *Super Trouper* by Abba? Is that not the most spooky coincidence you ever heard?

Tried to get back to sleep, but the house wouldn't let me. All those creaks and sighs and groans and squeaks turned my head into a blender. I imagined ghouls and ghosts lurking in the shadows waiting to chop me up! And every two minutes Mr E crashed through the cat flap and Napoleon went to sleep and fell off the back of the sofa. Between cat thump and cat flap I was in a state of nervous tension, and not even thinking angelic thoughts about Pamela Whitby could break this cycle of fear!

I passed a restless night.

SATURDAY

Was half-woken by the local paper dropping through the letterbox. Was fully woken by the front page. A picture of me with my finger poking through my pants and a headline that said: **WHO'S A WILLY LITTLE BOY THEN!**

This humiliation is William and Mel's fault. I don't care what the Revengers said about patience. I can no longer wait for revenge!

Mum and Dad never eat sugar, not even in tea. But my big brother and sister do. So I crept into the kitchen where somehow the sugar got knocked into the dustbin *by accident* and the bowl was refilled with salt.

The doorbell rang. It was Granny Constance, waving her copy of the local

THE TOOTING WORLD

WHO'S A WILLY LITTLE BOY THEN?

CONKERS

FAINTED

paper and shouting for Mum.

'It's eight o'clock in the morning!' she said, as Mum stumbled downstairs. 'It's practically the afternoon. Are you abandoning your children to bring *themselves* up, Celia?'

'Yes,' I said. 'It's a miracle we're normal.' Granny raised the rolled up newspaper and hit me on the legs. 'Ow!' I said. 'That hurt!'

'It was meant to,' she said. 'If I had my way I'd bring back the birch!'

'You'll feel better after a nice cup of tea,' Mum said. And she took Granny into the kitchen while I rubbed my bruises.

Suddenly I realized what she'd said.

'NO!' I shouted. 'NOT A CUP OF TEA!' I rushed into the kitchen just as Mum was spooning three spoons of salt into the old dragon's cup.

'Why not?' said Mum. 'Tea never killed anyone.'

'Here let me help you,' I said, grabbing Granny's cup and *by accident* chucking it out of the window. 'Oh dear and that was our last tea bag,' I said.

'No it wasn't,' said Mum.

'I meant tea . . . pot,' I said, sliding the teapot off the table and *by accident*

---

smashing it on the floor. 'That was our last teapot.'

'The boy has finally gone mad,' said Granny Constance.

'He's got a date this afternoon,' said Mum, as if that explained my behaviour, 'with a **G-I-R-L**.'

'Oh,' said Granny. 'That's the **E-N-D** of him then!'*

The phone rang and Granny answered it. 'It's the invalid,' she snapped to Mum. 'He

OOOOPS

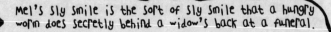

Mel's sly smile is the sort of sly smile that a hungry worm does secretly behind a widow's back at a funeral.

says he hasn't been fed yet, Celia. Must I do everything in this house?'

She took up Dad's breakfast and showed him the paper. He immediately summoned his family to his bedside.

'Alistair,' he sighed, as he took his cup of tea from Granny. 'Alistair, Alistair, Alistair . . .'

'Good morning, Daddy,' I said, while Mel smiled slyly.

'Alistair's a very naughty boy, isn't he?' she said.

Dad shook his head sadly and took a sip of his tea. That was the end of the lecture. His face went purple, the cup tipped over and boiling water splashed hotly down his front.

'What was that?' he howled.

'Hot tea with milk and sugar,' said Granny.

'He doesn't take sugar,' said Mum.

'Poison!' said William. 'Alistair's trying to kill him.'

'Don't be daft,' I replied. 'It was salt, meant for you two.'

Mum called an ambulance while Dad sent me to my room, but I couldn't get in because of Mel's clothes, so I stood on the landing like a lemon, not knowing what to do. I was still there when Dad was carried past on the stretcher.

'I'm not disobeying you,' I said. My voice was trembling. I felt really guilty about the salt in his tea. 'It's Mel's clothes, they're blocking the door.'

'Then clear them up,' he howled through gritted teeth. I felt so bad I did as I was told. And that's why I spent my morning – when I should have been getting ready for a hot date with Pamela Whitby – picking up and folding Mel's clothes!

Meeting Aaron in front of the cinema at 1.30. At 12.30 hid my yellow clothes inside the Scalextric box underneath my bed. Then instead of my canary suit put on my favourite jeans, favourite jumper and favourite trainers. Crept downstairs and had just opened the front door when Mel stepped out of the sitting room, where she'd obviously been waiting all week to ambush me. Then in a voice that was loud

enough for Dad to hear in the hospital burns unit, she screamed, 'Are you going now then, Alistair? Mummy's seen the way you're dressed has she?'

Death is too good for her! But flesh-eating scarab beetles burrowing through her body till they eat out her heart would go someway to making me feel better!

Mum sent me back to my room to change. I told her I couldn't find my yellow clothes, but William suggested I look inside the Scalextric box underneath my bed. Thank you, William.

When I was finally dressed, I stood in front of the mirror and was *maniacally* depressed. You know that numb feeling you get when you're standing in the middle of the road and a building's falling on your head and above you there's a jumbo jet about to crash and underneath your

feet there's an earthquake? Well, that's what I felt like. Picked on. I looked like a chicken drowning in custard.

Granny C + = ♡PAMELA♡

The disapproving look on Pamela Whitby's face when she saw my yellow clothes was everything I knew it would be. She looked just like Granny Constance sucking a lemon, only with more teeth. It turned out she'd also seen my candid photo in the *Tooting Tribune*. She hadn't wanted to come because of it. Apparently, she had strict rules about never associating with male strippers who showed their winkies in magazines, but she'd bought a new dress for the occasion so she had to come.

'And thank you, Alistair, for not saying how pretty I look in it,' she said.

'No problem,' I replied. She'd said thank you. Maybe I wasn't doing so badly after all!

'I didn't mean it,' she said.

'But I thought . . .'

'Anyone who thinks that the finger-willy thing is still funny when they're eleven is too immature for me,' she said.

'But it was my brother,' I told her.

'Ugh! You let your brother poke his finger out of your pants,' she said. 'Gross! You're even more of a disgustingly sick person than I thought you were earlier!'

That was in the foyer.

In the cinema, Ralph and Aaron kept winking at me and playing seat-frog until they managed to get Pamela Whitby and me sitting next to each other. But as the lights went down, my yellow clothes started glowing in the dark. I looked like a radioactive banana. I passed Pamela Whitby a note, saying: *I apologize for my appearance. Will never happen again.* But because of my bad hand-

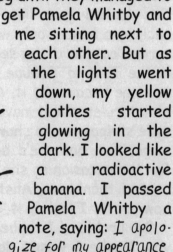

*From what I could hear, it was called *Doctor Voodoo* and was all about a snake-worshipping sect in Tahiti who took revenge on a wicked developer, who was trying to get them off their island, by scaring him with ancient woodland curses and voodoo black magic.

writing she read it as: *I assume both your parents were hippopotamuses.* So I got a slap round the ear, which meant I couldn't hear a word of the film.*

And Pamela Whitby turned her back on me and sighed with irritation everytime I looked at her.

After the film, I called a meeting of the Revengers in the gents loo. 'Marmalade cats like cream,' I said. 'Friends, you've got to help me! These last two days have been torture! My life is pants! I must have revenge.'

We looked up to see a man standing behind us. 'Sorry,' he said. 'I thought . . .'

I stepped forward. 'This loo is closed,' I said, 'by order of the police.'

'And we are the police,' said Ralph.

'CID,' said Aaron.

'What does that mean then?' he said.

'Child Investigation Department,' said Ralph.

'We're an anti-children crime squad,' I said, 'who check out small windows in public places to see if children can crawl through them to commit crime. Five minutes and we'll have the whole case sewn up!'

'Well get a move on,' he said. 'I'm busting.'

93

When we were alone again I listed my grievances.

1) Mum's betrayal on the yellow trouser front causing the Pamela Whitby slapping incident.
2) No grown-up allowance.
3) The embarrassing naked-finger photo.
4) Mel and William for being born.
5) The whole police threat thing that my big brother and sister had made happen with my rewriting *by accident* of Dad's will.

'There's a bounty on my head,' I said. 'I'm a wanted man.'

'Not by Pamela Whitby!' snorted Ralph. I ignored this wounding comment and asked the big question instead. What could we do?

'Voodoo,' said Aaron.

Blinding!

When we left the loo there was a queue of embarrassed men hopping up and down in the corridor. They all had damp trousers.

Dad is home from hospital. The doctor says

he needs a few days in bed to recover from the shock. Dad is taking it rather well. He's opened a bottle of champagne and is lying in bed, singing. He called me in. 'Thanks to your scalding,' he said, 'I really *can't* be there!'

'Where?' I said.

'Never you mind,' he laughed. 'Good work, son!' Then he gave me a huge kiss.

Kissing men is like kissing Mr E – stinky, wet and bristly. Kissing women however is like kissing warm jelly. I think I must be a jelly man. Only not with Granny Constance, because kissing Granny Constance is like kissing a bristly jelly made with antiseptic floor wash.

2.15 a.m. – Woken up by more spooky piano music outside my bedroom window.

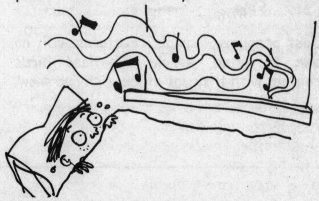

Suddenly thought it might be Pamela Whitby trying to make up for her stand-offishness today by serenading me under my window. Rushed to window and flung open curtain, but Pamela Whitby wasn't there. The music stopped too, and a car drove off with no lights. Spent the next twenty minutes trying to re-hang curtain on its rail.

It has not been my best day. Sometimes I wish I lived in an igloo on my own with no family, no girls, and no clothes.

I hate fish I really do

Just penguins – simple creatures with no axe to grind, simple flightless birds content with their lot of ice, fish and snow.

Nice

zzzZZZZUNDAY

I need my bedroom to myself. In one hour I am creating voodoo revenge magic against my evil family.

I knocked on Mel's door with my arms full of folded clothes. 'It's Sunday,' I shouted, but she was still asleep. I could hear her turning over in bed. 'You've got a date with Andy today.'

In a flash she was at the door in her pyjamas.* 'Oh brilliant,' she said, drowsily. 'Thanks for waking me, Alistair. I was meant to get up an hour ago to paint my nails.' She wasn't going to start being *nice* to me now, was she? She took her clothes with a smile and said, 'Thanks.' She *was*! I couldn't believe it. It wasn't fair! She couldn't suddenly be nice to me just as I was lining up the revenge of a lifetime!

So I tried to make her cross by shouting, 'Take your ugly black dress as well, you fat cowpat!' And threw the dress in her face, because I wanted her to hate me again so I could do evil things unto her without feeling guilty. But she was too fast asleep.

'Sorry,' she said. Then, 'Thanks again, Alistair.'

97

*That's not a door in her pyjamas. That's at the door wearing her pyjamas. If she'd had a door in her pyjamas she'd never get any sleep because people would be opening and closing the door all night. Unless it was a revolving door of course, but that wouldn't be much better, because you can trap your fingers in those.

BIG SISTERS!

You can't trust them to be nice
and you can't trust them
to be nasty.

The only thing you
can trust them to do is use
your razor to shave their legs!*

This morning, Dad had a hangover, but was still well-chuffed with his burns. 'A week off at least,' he grinned, as he waved William off to his rugby. 'Good luck, son, and remember, set and drive, half-breaks, and don't forget to shout from one to ten before kick-off. That's where the game's won. I'm proud of you!' He was crying when he turned round. Sport did that to him. He couldn't play it, but he sure could cry about it. When I called him a cry-baby, he looked quite upset and said it was the blisters rubbing against his bandages.

The Revengers arrived, and I impressed

bottom gas

on them the need to get our skates on where striking back was concerned. So after we'd hung a sign on the bedroom door that said

ENTER AT YOUR PERIL

- CURRIED EGG EATING

CONTEST -

LETHAL GAS LEAK

we got straight down to it. Or rather we would have done if Mel hadn't suddenly burst in.

'You little toad,' she screamed. 'Look at the creases in my black dress! If I'm not ready for Andy when he comes you'll pay big time. Every time you're in the loo for the next five years I'll switch off the light! I hate you, Alice! I wish you'd never been born! And I'm *not* a fat cowpat!' She slammed the door as she left.

The other two Revengers were shocked at what she'd said, but I was delighted. 'Everything's back to normal,' I said, rubbing my hands. 'Shall we proceed with the punishment?'

We decided to make three voodoo dolls. 'How do we do that?' said Aaron.

'I don't know,' I said. 'It's a shame they never made voodoo dolls on *Blue Peter*, isn't it?' I stood up to demonstrate. '*Hello, children. Today we're making a fully-working, black magic voodoo doll. And all you'll need is a used washing-up liquid bottle, an old sock, the evil eye of Schamane, some sticky-back plastic and a dozen ordinary pins. Can you do voodoo? Let's find out!*

'But that's brilliant,' said Ralph. 'That *is* how we do it.'

We found some old stuff in the bin in the kitchen and assembled it back in my bedroom. Mum's doll had a squeezy bottle for a body, pipe-cleaners for arms and legs, an old tennis ball for a head and string for hair. Then we painted **MUM** on the front so we wouldn't get muddled.

100

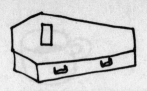

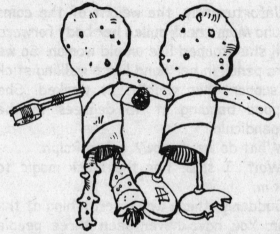

The bodies of Mel and William's dolls were made from old loo rolls. Their heads were potatoes. One of Mel's legs was a carrot while the other was an asparagus. Her arms were a toothbrush and one of Granny's half-smoked cigars. William's arms were Peperamis and his legs were the glass stems from two broken wineglasses.

Then for the magic. I wanted Mum to be less mean with her money and give me more, so we put three pennies in an Action Man saddlebag and hung it round her neck. William and Mel's punishment was less specific. I just wanted to cause them pain generally, so we stuck six sewing pins into their potatoes and loo rolls.

Unfortunately, the weight of the coins around Mum's neck pulled her body forward until she stooped like an old woman. So we put a pencil in her hand like a walking stick to support her weight. It worked. She stopped bending at 45 degrees to the perpendicular.

'What do we do now?' asked Ralph.

'Wait,' I said. 'For the black magic to kick in.'

Suddenly, there was a scratching at the door. You have never seen three people jump out their skins like we did. We thought it was an evil spirit or a gremlin at the very least, but the fur we saw flash through the door belonged to Napoleon. He padded across the floor ignoring us in that superior nose-in-the-air way he has. Then, to our horror, he jumped up onto the desk where the dolls were standing. I could see it coming. A clumsy landing, two paws up in the air whoompf! Napoleon fell over, taking William and Mel's dolls with him. Mel's doll was lucky. It just fell head first into a mug of cold, milky tea, but William's doll rolled off the desk and smashed one of its legs on the floor.

'Oops!' I said. 'What have we done?'

The doorbell rang and we found out.

It was William. He was still wearing his rugby kit. In his hands he had two crutches. On his leg a white plaster! 'It's a hairline fracture of my ankle,' he said in a tiny tearful voice. 'I've never been injured before.'

I turned to the Revengers.

Spooooky!

Because of William's leg, Aaron and Ralph were sent home and lunch was delayed until 4.00. This sent Mel into a tizz, because Andy was picking her up in his passion-wagon at 5.30. And because she was in her new black dress, full make-up, coiffed-up hair and tights and jewellery and everything she couldn't possibly help to carry, or serve, or talk, or pass the mustard, or do anything human, really. She was a bag of bad-tempered nerves, who got away with being rude, because as Mum said, 'It's a very stressful night for her.'*

Anyway, neither Mel nor William could walk, so Muggins had to do all the fetching from the kitchen. I don't know what happened. One moment the jug of milk was safely in my hand the next I was flying. I screamed, 'Look out!' As Mel turned to see  what I was shouting about, the milk jug dumped its load in her face. The milk soaked her hair, poured down her neck and covered her little black dress in a big white stain. The silence was electric. I couldn't move, Mel couldn't move, William couldn't move and Dad was upstairs in bed.

Mum reacted first. She picked me up by the seat of my pants and said, 'You stupid selfish little boy!'

'It was an accident!' I cried. They didn't believe me. 'No it was, this time it was! I really *didn't* mean to do it. A huge ghostly hand pushed me in the back and I tripped. Honestly it did!'

The doorbell rang and Mel snapped out of her trance. She burst into tears and ran out the room dripping milk. 'I don't want to see him!' she wailed. So Mum had to tell Andy that Mel was sick and I was sent to my room again. I wouldn't have minded if I'd done it deliberately, but I hadn't. Something supernatural had pushed me!

Double-spooooky!

But back in my bedroom I saw something that made my heart stop in terror. The pencil had slipped out of pipe cleaner and gravity had done its worst on the washing-up liquid bottle. Mum's doll was bent double. Her head was touching her knees! What in the name of the sacred jujube tree was going to happen to *her*?

Heard a scraping behind me and turned in a panic. A note had been pushed under my door.

> This is war. And like you, war is ugly. We will not be taking prisoners.
> M+W

Suddenly, there was a scream from downstairs. With my heart in my mouth, I rushed into the kitchen to find Mum bent double over the washing-up.

'I've put my back out,' she cried, 'picking up this pencil!'

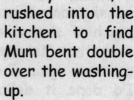

Triple-spooooky!

Had another weird dream.

My Another Weird Dream

My dad dies of slothfulness. He's attacked in bed by a sloth and smothered to death. But a witch doctor wearing Mel's little black dress raises Dad from the dead with a glass of milk so he can point out his murderer. He points to me. And suddenly I realize I'm standing in a courtroom in a big furry sloth costume and the judge is Mum with a tennis ball head. Then Mel and William stand up in the dock wearing army uniforms, and promise to fight Alice Fury till he acknowledges them as superior beings with more right to breathe air than him. And the judge seems pleased, only it's not the judge anymore, it's Granny Constance waving a bunch of twigs, and she tells me to bend over and pull down my trousers . . .

That was when I woke up. I'm awake now and can hear the house breathing again. Those dreaded noises of the night. Cracks and creaks and scrapes and squeaks and gurgling groans like the Devil. Am I going mad, dear diary? If someone up there thinks this is funny, I've got news for you, mate – it's not!

Today has been the freakiest day of my life. It started this morning. Strange goings-on had been going on all night. The clothes I'd put away for Mel had been thrown out of her cupboard onto the landing. She blamed me, but why would I want to do all that picking up and folding again? Dad's will was stolen from William's room,* put into an envelope and left on the hall table addressed to the police. And Napoleon the tail-less cat walked along the banisters *without* falling off!

In the First Year loos at school, I shared my worst fears with the Revengers. 'We've stirred up evil,' I said. 'We've opened the black magic box and now we can't close it again!'

'No,' said Ralph. 'It's Mel and William mucking about, trying to scare you.'

'No, it can't be,' I said. 'William

*where he'd been hiding it in case he needed to blackmail me.

can't move anywhere unless he's on crutches and they make a thumping noise so I'd have heard him!'

'It can't be real, because they weren't real voodoo dolls,' said Aaron. 'They were made out of rubbish.'

'But I've seen the miracle with my own eyes. Guys! For once, Napoleon *didn't* fall of the banisters. He's cured! He can walk again!'

When we left the loos after the meeting there was a line of First Years waiting to go.

'Oh my God!' I gasped.

'What?' said the others.

'There!' I said, pointing to the freaky dryness. 'No wet trousers! That proves it!' Aaron and Ralph nodded their heads and smiled at me like doctors do just before they strap you into a straitjacket!

But the worst was yet to come. When I got home Dad was out of bed. Him and Mum were waiting in the kitchen. As I shut the front door they called me through, and with her walking frame, Mum pointed to her new shiny copper hood. Scratched across the front with a nail, in shaky letters 50 cm high, was the word

ALICE

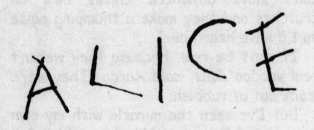

'I didn't do it,' I squeaked.

'Then who did?' seethed Mum. 'It's *your* name.'

'It's not my name! I'm not called Alice. I'm Alistair. I'm a boy. I didn't do it!'

'Fifteen hundred pounds!' exploded my dad, clutching his burns. 'Now you've gone and burst my blisters again, you stupid boy!'

'It must be them,' I said, as Mel and William walked in. 'Tell them you did it.'

My big brother and sister looked at each other and laughed.

'Why would we do this?' said Mel. 'Maybe it's the ghost!'

'What ghost?' said Mum.

The blood drained from my face. 'The ghost I keep hearing every night,' I whispered. Had Mel heard it too?

Then suddenly,

CRASH!

The back door burst open and Mr E was standing outside with his front paws and face plastered black with mud. He took one look at me, yelped, bit my hand and charged outside like he'd just been stung on the bum by a bee.

'Dog's are sensitive to spirits,' said Mel. 'Did anyone else hear Mr E howling at the moon last night?'

'Me,' said William, 'at midnight when the beasts of Beelzebub scavenge for souls!'

'Stop it!' said Mum. 'You're scaring Alistair.'

'No they're not,' I lied.*

'Well, if you're petrified tonight, Alistair, I'm only next door,' said Mel. 'All you have to do is scream . . . if the bogeyman hasn't slit your throat first!'

Mum sent all three of us to bed. She's bad-tempered because of her back. Mind you, if I had to smell my cheesy feet all day I think I might be bad-tempered too. I've

straightened her doll. Let's hope it works.

4.00 a.m. – I haven't slept a wink. This house is throbbing with supernatural phenomena. I've heard clanking chains, thumping footsteps, mournful wailing, ghostly laughter and a wettish sort of splattering in the garden! Why did I do this? If I get out of this alive I shall never do revenges ever again.
Well maybe one or two

I've only gone and summoned up the dark demons of Ghede and got us haunted!

What was that noise? There was a knocking on my wall! There's something *in* there behind the wallpaper! It's only a matter of time before that door bursts open and a wild-haired, sabre-toothed thing with a hound's head and a goat's body snatches me into the fiery pits where I'll roast in Hell for time everlasting!
I wonder if Mum depriving me of food by sending me to bed without supper has affected my brain?

Is liver the most disgusting meat ever invented?

Mum woke me up. She has doubled in size since last night, but do I get thanked?

Scared to come out of my bedroom. Expecting to see blood up the walls and severed limbs stuck to the carpet, but when I did venture out it wasn't as nasty as that. The loo has been vandalized. The chain is missing. We have passed a hose pipe through the window so that we can flush at our convenience.

While we were in the garden sorting the hose I couldn't help noticing that the lawn was covered in bones. Mr E thought he'd died and gone to Heaven. 'Where do these come from?' I said.

'From inside our bodies,' said William. 'Have you never heard of bones? They join together to make a skeleton.'

'Ha ha!' I said. 'I'm not stupid.'

'Oh sorry,' he said. 'I thought you were.'

'I meant, how did they get on the grass?'*

Later at school, Aaron pointed to the ground with a shaking finger and said softly, 'I know where the bones came from.' We all looked down. Then we all looked up again with eyes as wide as saucers. The end of Aaron's nose was twitching. 'Who's seen the film *Poltergeist*?' he trembled.

'You don't mean . . .' Ralph didn't dare say it, but I did.

'My house is built on a graveyard? So those bones are the bones of the dead!'

'Who we've woken up!' gasped Aaron. 'They're climbing out their coffins!'

'And when they've climbed into your garden they'll join up and turn themselves into a huge army of murdering skeletons!' squawked Ralph. Only he squawked it a bit too loud, because Miss Bird heard.

'I've warned you three before,' she said. 'Tomorrow. After school. Detention!'

eat. It would fall off your fork all the time, being as it is, the size of a rat's dropping. I should add that if he brain was any bigger he would not be allowed to play rugby.

There was only one way to find out if my house was built on top of a graveyard full of zombies.

12.00 a.m. midnight – I put a handkerchief across Mr E's yappy mouth and tied him to the fridge. Aaron and Ralph were waiting for me in the garden. We all had torches and spades, although Aaron's was a plastic one from a beach set.

'We don't have a garden,' he said. 'Mum grows carrots in a window box, but she doesn't need a spade for that.'

'How many carrots do you get in a window box?' I asked.

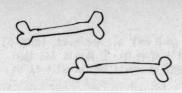

'Three,' he said. 'Small ones. I must have dug them up too soon, but I wanted to see how they were growing.'

Ralph produced a bottle of lemonade, only it wasn't lemonade. 'It's holy water,' he said. 'I nicked it out the bird bath in the garden. Before we start we've got to splash it all over to protect us from the buried-bad-things.'

We splashed the water all over our faces and hands and everywhere else by mistake. 'Has anyone got a towel?' asked Aaron. But we hadn't, so we dug wet.

1.00 a.m. – We were exhausted. We'd dug so many little holes in the lawn that they'd joined up into one large one. We found a few things from the house that Mr E had buried, like Mum's glasses, a pink sock and the TV remote, but no graveyard. It was a relief in one way but a worry in another. We still didn't know what was causing all this spookiness.

2.00 a.m. – Back in bed.

3.00 a.m. – I am never sleeping ever again! Half an hour ago, a figure appeared at the end of my bed. I couldn't see his face because he was wearing a hood, but he had something in his hand. It was a long pole that he thumped on the ground when he walked.

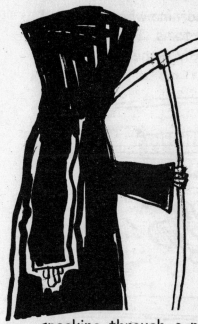

It was only after he'd been there a few seconds that I realized who it was. It was Death, the Grim Reaper and the thumping was his wooden scythe that he uses to harvest souls! His voice rattled like he was speaking through a paper and comb, but because this was Death I knew I was just imagining that. He said, 'Now you're for it, Alice Fury. Sleeping bones should be left to lie, but you wouldn't. Don't go to sleep tonight or you'll never wake up again!'

*or should I say 'what'?

I screamed so loud that Death ran away, but nobody came to my rescue. I fled into Mum and Dad's bedroom, but he was snoring and she had more tissues in her ears. I thought parents were supposed to be loving and protective.*

117

WEDNESDAY

Bit of trouble this morning when Mum and Dad opened their curtains. Their precious lawn had mysteriously vanished. In its place was a crater.

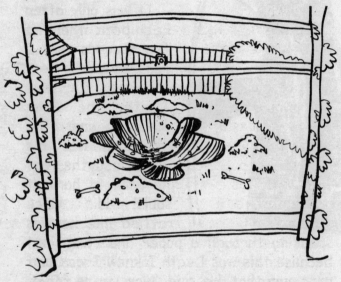

'Who did this?' wept Dad. 'I'm trying to get better here. Trying to get back to work to support my family. Then this comes along, and I think what's the point?'

'You're upset,' I said. 'Sit down.'

'I'm not upset,' Dad shouted. 'I'm angry, Alistair. Who could have done this to us?'

'Moles?' I said. 'I've heard that moles like a good party.'

'This mess is not moles partying,' said Dad coldly.

'A spaceship?' I suggested. 'As it lands, the blast from its rocket blows a hole in your lawn.'

'So where is this spaceship then?' asked William. He makes things worse deliberately. He loves watching me squirm. If he'd just let me lie without butting in everything would be all right!

'The spaceship is in another garden,' I said. 'It probably bounced on landing.'

'This is not a blast from a spaceship,' said Dad. 'This is digging.'

'Then maybe it's Mr E,' I said. 'It's not me. In fact I'm sure it's Mr E, because I found these in the kitchen this morning,' and I produced the glasses, the sock and the remote. That did the trick. They believed me.

But here's the problem – *I* know it's not true! Just as I know what *is* true; i.e. the bones, the rattling chains, the thumping walls and the Grim Reaper! I'm cursed!

'All houses make noises,' Mum said when I told her what I was scared of. 'Pipes clang, radiators gurgle, floorboards creak. That's what you're hearing.'

*I was lucky not to get a gash in my knee, because right next to the marrow in the woman's shopping bag was a glass jar of French mustard. If my knee had gone into that I could have cut it to shreds!

'Or maybe not,' said Mel. 'Maybe all this spookiness is something to do with Dad's illness,' she went on. 'Maybe what he was coughing up last week was ectoplasm. Maybe that's why he can't get better, because this ghost is feeding off his brain and as Dad gets weaker the ghost gets stronger, until finally Dad pops his clogs and the ghost takes his place!'

At the thought of Dad's skull being sucked inside out, I freaked. I ran down the stairs screaming. I ran out the front door screaming. I ran down the road screaming. And I only stopped screaming when I fell over a pushchair and squashed a marrow with my knee.*

'Sorry,' I said. 'I'm being chased by a ghost!'

The woman recognized my uniform and

120

reported me to the school. Got another detention to go along with the one I already had. When Miss Bird turned up to supervise me I asked her if I could do both together.

'With pleasure, 'she said. 'There's nothing I like better than a double detention.'

'Me neither,' I said. I didn't tell her I was too scared to go home.

Before I could start writing out Mum's recipes I just *had* to ask. 'Did you taste any of the recipes I copied last time?' I said.

'I did,' she said.
'And how were they?'

'Delicious,' she said. Delicious! Stinging nettles, chicken's feet, pork fat, leaves and mouse! She must have taste buds like steel rivets!

'Yes, delicious,' she said. 'I found one

But then I always thought she was a robot.

121

or two of the ingredients hard to read because of your handwriting but I worked them out in the end.' She handed me the recipes I'd copied out last time. The page was full of her corrections.

~~a handful of stinging nettles~~
a handful of steaming noodles
~~two large chicken's feet~~
two large chicory roots
~~left-over pork fat~~
left-over port wine
~~nine tablespoons of finely chopped leaves~~
nine tablespoons of finely diced leeks
~~chopped mouse~~
chocolate mousse

So there it was. She couldn't read my handwriting. All that cunning work for nothing. But there again, if she couldn't read what I'd written it didn't matter what I wrote. So this time I went mad and in amongst the recipes I hid the following ingredients: the cremated remains of a beloved pet; a litre of virgin engine oil; curdled cream scraped from the dustbin; chipmunk wee; frog spawn; six tablespoons of ear wax; a plate of unwashed socks; half a centipede and the gunk-encrusted toe jam from a tortoise.

I am so embarrassed

TOE JAM CREAM

Got home late to find Mel and William waiting for me in the sitting room with a woman called Talia. She was all earrings and red hair. Her green dress had swirly patterns on and matched the rug in the hall.

'Oh, you're a boy,' she said. 'I thought your sister said your name was Alice.'

'I have conkers,' I said. 'Why were you talking to my sister?'

'She thinks you might be causing the hauntings,' she said. 'But be not afraid, for I am here to help.'

Talia was a psychic medium. She went into a trance to find out why we were being haunted. It was like watching a cow with BSE. She shook her head, waved her arms, fell down and foamed at the mouth. Then suddenly, she rolled back her eyes and said in a voice that was clearly not her own,* 'Hello. I'm a ghost and I've got a message for Alice . . . stair, I mean.'

Everyone gasped. How had the ghost known my name?

Talia suddenly snapped out of her trance and wiped the foam off her chin. 'Well that clearly indicates a presence, Alistair, but I'm not surprised because psychic disturbance is always channelled through the youngest boy in a family, which is you.'

'And the cure?' asked Mel.

'An exorcism,' said Talia. 'An exorcist must be found forthwith. Ooh, hang on!' Suddenly her eyes snapped shut again. 'I'm getting some-thing else,' she said. 'Oh no! No, it can't be!'

'What?' I said.

'Death!' she shouted. 'Death! Death! Death!' She made such a racket that Mum and Dad rushed in. 'I see imminent Death in the family!' Dad immediately assumed it was him and had a fit.

'It's me, isn't it?' he wailed. 'I *am* going to die! I *am* going to die!'

And all I could think about was that stupid will! 'And I'm going to prison!' I screamed.

The room fell silent. 'Why?' said Mum and Dad together. 'What have you done now?'

Before I could answer, the phone rang. Great Uncle Crawford is dead.

When I first heard the news I jumped up and down and hugged Dad, and both of us cheered, because it *wasn't* Dad who was dead! But then we remembered that Great Uncle Crawford *was* dead, which was very sad, so we started acting sorry and trying to cry, even though neither of us produced a single tear.

I know why I couldn't cry. We're going to Ireland tomorrow for the funeral on Friday. That means I'm missing my piano lesson again! Hallelujah!

When I say *we're* going to Ireland, that's everyone except Dad. He says the shock has made his scald worse, and besides he read somewhere that flying can make a sick man explode.

'Don't worry about me,' he croaked. 'I'll

stay behind and try to get better all on my own.'

That mean's he's going to drink beer again. And Mum knows it. I can tell from her tight lips.

When Mum's mouth is pinched it looks exactly like Napoleon's bottom

Have never seen a dead body before. In Ireland they don't have lids on their coffins, because when they throw a party for the dead person they want the corpse to be able to get up and dance. If that happens while I'm in the room, I'm on the first plane home.

THURSDAY

Before we left for Ireland, Mum phoned Miss Bird and said I wouldn't be in for the next couple of days.

'That's fine,' said Miss Bird, 'but tell Alistair that his punishment is Saturday morning detentions, starting this weekend, for as long as it takes till he's finished the recipes.'

'Finished the recipes?' said Mum.

'I mean caught up with his lessons,' said Miss Bird. 'Sorry! Soup of the tongue.'

Did I not swear I would never go shopping with my mum again?

We got to Heathrow airport and she said, 'Did you bring a suit?'

I said, 'No.'

'Why not?' she shrieked.

'I don't own one,' I said.

'Everyone wears a suit to a funeral,' she said, and before I could complain she'd dragged me into the nearest men's store, pulled a black suit off the peg and told me to drop my trousers.

'I won't do it,' I said. 'Look at the trouble I got into last time. If you want me to try that suit on, I'm doing it in the changing room.'

'Fine,' she hissed, 'but hurry up or we'll miss the plane.'

Felt safer in the cubicle. It had a floor-to-ceiling curtain. Not that it made any difference. I was wearing the suit jacket and had just dropped my jeans to put the trousers on, when I heard a loud cheer from the other side of the curtain, followed by a shrill blast of party trumpets

and the pop of champagne.

'Oh,' I thought to myself, 'It must be a member of staff's birthday.' Wrong! The curtain was whipped back by a man I'd never seen before. I tried to cover my pants with my hands but my palms were too small. Behind this grinning stranger were hundreds of people with glasses of champagne and paper streamers round their necks.

'Smile,' said a sweaty man with a camera. The flash went off in my face and everyone cheered. I was the millionth customer in the store and my great and glorious prize was to have my face and my pants on the front of every in-flight magazine on every plane that left Heathrow for the next ten years! Not only that, but this particular men's store had branches in every High Street in the country. So my picture was going nation-wide as well.

'Well, thanks,' I said to my mum.*

'Never mind,' she said. 'We got the suit free and at least this time you didn't have your finger sticking out your pants.'

'Didn't need to,' said William.

'What do you mean?' I said, as a hot flush rushed up my body. If it wasn't my finger . . .

Arrived at the cottage in Dunboyne outside Dublin, where Great Uncle Crawford was laid out in his coffin. Worst

Please, please, please don't let this have happened!

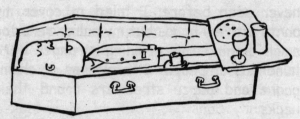

luck, the coffin *didn't* have a lid. Mum had to push me into the room where it was lying on top of the kitchen table. There were bottles and crisps and half-eaten sandwiches all round it and someone had put a sausage roll in Great Uncle Crawford's hand. He was as pale as a waxwork. He looked like eating that sausage roll might make him feel better.

Everyone was very friendly with drink, and they all wanted to know where Dad was. Mum had told us on the plane that we were just to say he was ill so as not to cause offence.

'Ill,' said Mum.

'How ill?' said Granny Constance. 'When I saw him on Saturday he wasn't too bad.'

'Very ill,' said Mum.

'He's going to die!' wailed my granny.*

'No, he's not,' said Mum.

'So what exactly has he got then?' asked Dad's sour-faced sister, Andrea. 'What has

130

he got that prevents him from hopping on an aeroplane like the rest of us and making an effort to see his own flesh and blood?'

Mum hesitated so I jumped in.

'Rabies,' I said.

Granny Constance gasped. Mum looked astonished. William and Mel groaned like I'd just let the side down again.

'They don't let you out of the country with rabies,' I said. It wasn't fair. I was only trying to help. Now everyone was staring at me.

'Dear God,' said Granny. 'The poor boy. How did he catch that?'

'Off the postman,'
I said.

'The postman!'

'Who'd been bitten by a dog,' I added. Everything I said made it worse.

'Do the Post Office know?' asked Andrea's partner, Graham.

'Oh yes,' I said. 'They've put the dog down.'

'Have they?' he said. 'And the postman?'

'*And* the postman,' I said. 'Both of them at the same time. Double shot.' William and Mel put their heads in their hands. 'But

Dad was lucky apparently. He hasn't got the   foam-at-the-mouth-and-turn-into-a-mad-fox type of rabies, he's just got the type of rabies where you can't fly to Ireland and see your family and you must stay in bed . . . watching telly.'

The thing about lying is some people are really good at it whereas I'm not. Nobody spoke to me for the rest of the day. I think they thought I was a little soft in the head.

Sat in the corner of the room watching everyone get drunk and dance to a fiddle and William's paper and comb. They were stuffing their faces with snacks and pies that Granny kept laying out alongside the coffin. Had plenty of time to think and was thinking, if there was a power failure and everyone was groping for food in the dark, what if I ate a finger by mistake thinking it was a carrot baton?*

Also I swear that Great Uncle Crawford was watching me. His eyes never left me all night. It was like they wanted something from me.

That night, William, Mel and I slept in one big bed. Mum was in another room. After my big brother and sister had told me a hundred times how stupid I was to open my mouth on the rabies thing, they took all the duvet and left me to freeze on the edge of the bed. The cold made me want the loo, so I got out of bed and put my foot in a metal bucket. The noise of me clumping around the room trying to shake off the bucket woke William and Mel.

'What are you doing?' they moaned.

'I'm trying to go to the loo, but it's dark and I don't know the way.'

'See that thing on your foot,' said Mel.

'This bucket?' I said.

'That is the loo,' she said. 'It's a potty.' No way was I going to the loo in *that*, not with my foot in it and not with Mel and William listening either!

Hopped back into bed and hung on.

As I lay there next to my big brother and sister, unable to sleep, listening to the night, I realized something. This cottage in

They'd probably record it and play it back to Pamela Whitby or something!

Ireland made scarier noises than our house in England; the wind outside that never stopped whining, the staircase that creaked like old bones, the roof that rustled with rats! But I wasn't scared. What was missing, as I lay there next to my big brother and sister, were the other noises, the thumping, the rattling, the eerie voices through the wall. As I lay there next to my big brother and sister a dim little light flickered to life in the back of my head.

4.30 a.m. – If they don't have a loo here with a flush and everything, maybe the burial's going to be a bit backward too. Maybe there'll just be four big men, two on the legs and two on the arms, swinging Great Dead Uncle Crawford's stiff little body as far away from the house as they can chuck it!

It is the morning of the funeral. I'm sitting up in bed. I'm worried I don't feel sad. If it's compulsory to cry at a funeral I'm in big trouble.

William and Mel had got all of the duvet again so slid out of bed to put on my clothes before I froze to death. Only I couldn't find them. I looked on the chair where I'd left them, under the chair, behind the chair, on the ceiling above the chair, but they weren't there. My new suit, my shirt, socks and black school shoes had disappeared! Only two people could have done this.

'Where is it?' I said.

'What?' said Mel.

'My suit. Ha-ha, hee-hee! My sides are split-ting! I'm only standing here with frostbite, aren't I?'

I wish I'd brought an onion.

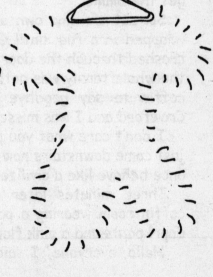

135

'We don't know,' said William. 'Why would I want your suit anyway? I've got one of my own.'

When Mum found out she was furious. She said I'd deliberately lost my suit, because I hated it. And I wasn't wearing my jeans and showing her up. It was the suit or nothing.

William sniggered as he straightened his tie. 'So what are you going to wear? Bath mat? Curtain? Yellow trousers?'

Nothing. If I couldn't find my clothes I wasn't going. And when Mum found out that Mel and William had hidden them *they'd* get the blame.

So sat on my own in the bedroom, wrapped in a rug, until Granny Constance crashed through the door and told me that the whole family was gathered around the coffin to say goodbye to Great Uncle Crawford and I was missed.

'I don't care what you put on,' she spat,' just come downstairs now, Alistair, and for once behave like a civilized human being!'

Three minutes later walked into the coffin room wearing a pair of Mum's red Capri pants and a pink flowery blouse.

'Hello, everyone,' I said. 'I'm Alistair in

case you think I'm Mum. I'm sorry I'm late, but I've lost my sui . . .'

And then I saw it. It was wrapped around the dead body. Great Uncle Crawford was wearing it!

'I thought I heard footsteps coming up the stairs last night,' William whispered in my ear.

'Talia was right,' said Mel. 'You're a supernatural magnet. What with every-thing spooky at home and now this! If I were you, Alistair, I'd be very afraid.'

I was. I was very, very, VERY afraid! Because of me, the dead were walking!

While I stood terrified in the doorway, four men pushed past me and started to nail down the coffin lid. Mum rushed forward and hurled herself across the corpse like a grieving widow. Only she wasn't grieving. She was stripping the little old man of his clothes and handing them to me.

'Now you can nail it down,' she said to the undertakers, who stared at Mum like she was the meanest woman in the world for sending a man to his grave in his pants!

Then she told me to put my clothes on quickly or the funeral cars would have to go without me.

'I'm not wearing these,' I said, dropping the clothes on the floor. 'There's been a dead man in them! They're fish-cold! Feel them.'

But Granny Constance was in no mood for arguments. 'If you don't put them on,' she said, 'I'll bury you with Crawford!'

After wearing the clothes for ten minutes they didn't seem quite so cold. I opened the window of the limousine to let the smell of death escape and by the time we reached the church, the suit was almost comfortable. I say *almost* because I found a foreign fingernail in one of the pockets that made my flesh creep.

After the service the whole family stood around a hole in the graveyard while Great Uncle Crawford's coffin was lowered into the ground. This was when most people cried. Even William and Mel had their heads in their hands, so I copied what they were doing and jiggled my shoulders up and down to make it look like I was weeping.*

It was while I had my head lowered that I saw the dog under the tree. He was digging a hole in an old grave when suddenly he fell in and disappeared. Seconds later he re-emerged with several bones in his

4

mouth. Then he ran over towards us, dropped them into Great Uncle Crawford's grave and went back for more. There was an embarrasses shuffling by the graveside as the family wondered what to do.

The priest was very good and tried to put everyone at their ease by cracking a funny joke. 'Well, Crawford will not be short of a nice drop of soup in the after-life!' he said to complete silence. Then realizing he'd made a bit of a blunder, he kicked the dog away and ordered the gravediggers to chuck in the soil to cover the bones from view.

But I had had a revelation. Bones and soup and dogs and graveyards! The Revengers had been looking for a grave-yard under the garden, but it was just Mum's soup bones that Mr E had dragged out the shed and scattered on the lawn. And if those terrifying bones weren't terrifying bones at all, then who was to say that the hauntings I heard every night weren't perfectly explainable too? Because there weren't any haunting noises last night. Not last night when Mel and William were sleeping in the same room as me and couldn't get out to *make* the noises!

Looked at Mel and William and realized they weren't crying at all. They were giggling.

It all makes sense now! How could I have been such a clump? Mum's new copper hood was scratched by a nail – one of Mel's nails that she'd stuck on for Andy! The Grim Reaper's scythe and his paper and comb voice – it was William on crutches! The clanking chain – that came from the loo. The scratching, the footsteps, the wailing, the laughter, the tapping on the wall – they were all Mel and William, paying me back for the voodoo dolls!

I am full of rage. To think how my mind has been twisted by terror that wasn't terror at all. This treachery by my big brother and sister demands a payback of humungous proportions! I shall not write anything else for a while. I must reserve my brainpower for the thinking up of evil.

Oh come, Revengers, come to me and we shall stuff them up big time!

FRIDAY NIGHT

We're at the airport flying home. William and Mel do not suspect that I know a thing. I am hiding in the airport loos so that Mum cannot take me on another shopping spree. I think they're calling my flight.

FRIDAY NIGHT @ HOME

When we got home, Mum found Dad in bed with a crate of beer.

'I wasn't expecting you home so early,' he said to Mum, trying to hide the bottles under his pillow.

Mum slept in the sitting room. There was a note on my bed from Dad.

Mad Mrs Muttley phoned. Lock your windows and doors, son. She sounded slightly detached from reality.
Dad

SATURDAY

Woke up in my own bed. It's a weird day outside. It's swirling with fog and the street lamps are glowing yellowy-orange like firemen's torches in a blaze.

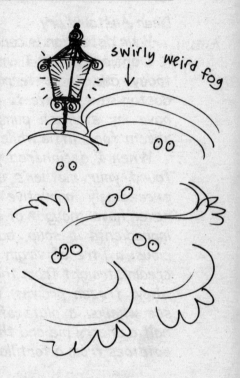

swirly weird fog

Mum and Dad are still not talking. Dad is pretending he's really ill again to make Mum feel sorry for him and forgive him his trespasses. But she's not happy that he pretended to be more ill than he really was just to get out of going to Ireland, so he could drink beer and watch sport uninterrupted.

Phoned Aaron and Ralph last night and they are coming round later this morning after I have done my detention for Pigeon.

Got to school to find this note pinned to the detention room door:

*Double yesssssss! She must have read my handwriting and cooked up some of my ingredients!

**So why's she in hospital if she's misread my disgusting ingredients as edible ones?

Dear Alistair Fury,

yesssssss   *Your detention is cancelled.*

I apologize, but I am unable to come in today due to a terrible sickness. The doctor says I have to go into hospital to have my stomach pumped, so I may be absent for a little while longer.*

When I deciphered your handwriting I found your mother's use of ingredients exceedingly innovative and bold. I would never have thought of using the following ingredients in soup, but they were delicious: a litre of virgin endive oil; clotted cream straight from the dairyman; cheesy whey; frozen prawns; six tablespoons of sea whelks; a plate of unwasted stocks; half a cherry pie and the burnt and crusty potatoes from a tortilla.**

Yours faithfully,
Miss Bird
    P.S. I miss my pet cat dreadfully, but she certainly livened up a leek and potato broth.

Ugh! Now I feel sick.
The feeling got worse when I arrived home to find Mrs Muttley sitting at the

144

kitchen table. Slammed hands into pockets to hide fingers. She was crying and eating a whole packet of chocolate digestive biscuits. Mum was holding her hand.

'Do you like me teaching you the piano, Alistair?' blubbed Mrs Muttley. Her red wet cheeks wobbled with emotion. 'Only I'm not stupid. If you lose your fingers in a lawn mower accident you don't just *forget* to tell your piano teacher. I think you don't like me.'

'Look,' I cried, whipping out my fingers and wiggling them. 'It's a miracle. A surgeon just made me a new lot out of carrots and glue!'

excellent

But Mrs Muttley was no fool. She knew that carrots wouldn't work as fingers. One sniff of a cheese and chive dip and they'd be totally out of control. 'I've tried to make you love the piano,' she sobbed. 'I even came round a few nights ago and played Beethoven on the car stereo outside your bedroom window. I thought it might inspire you.' So that was the ghostly *Phantom* music that nearly scared me to death! This woman was a psycho! 'I don't want to lose you, Alistair. So I'm going to ask this question once and never again. Do you want to carry on playing the piano? If you say no I'll walk away and you'll never see me again, but if you say yes . . .' She looked at me with puppy dog eyes. '. . . if you say yes, you'll be rich and famous and own a yacht!'

I'll be honest here. Even though I knew she'd been practising that speech all the way over in the car, and only wanted me back for the sake of the £10 note I paid her every week, I still couldn't help being flattered. 'Wow, stardom!' I said. 'Yeah, sure! I'll carry on!' My one big chance to escape from tinkling her ivories and I blew it!

Later the Revengers came round for a Council of War. First we did the swearing in.

'I'm b***dy well going to kill them!'

'So am b***dy I.'

'And b***dy me!'

Then we sat around on the Carpet of War and discussed strategies. Ralph was all for tying bricks to Mel and William's shoes and chucking them in the river.

Aaron couldn't see the point. 'What harm have their shoes ever done us?' he said. 'I mean what's the point in drowning their shoes?'

'I was rather assuming that they'd be in them,' said Ralph.

'No,' I said. 'Not murder. They've been spooking me, so we've got to spook them back.'

'Well,' said Aaron, 'don't laugh, but I think this might work. We hire a pantomime horse costume and two of us get in it. Then the third one of us sits on top wearing a polo necked jumper which he pulls up over his head so it looks like he's headless. Then we ride around the garden wailing "whoo" and "waah".'

'I thought horses went neigh,' said Ralph.

'I was being the ghost,' said Aaron.

'I know,' said Ralph. We were getting nowhere fast.

Thinking up a haunting revenge was not as easy as it sounds. We bashed our brains together to think of a way for one of us to walk through a wall. That would be scary. But the only way we could think of walking through a wall was by using a door, and that

it's no good, it's locked

was pretty ordinary and not scary at all. Unless the door led to a room full of vampires or funnel web spiders, but we didn't have any of those.

After an hour of not having any good ideas, the doorbell rang. I went out onto the landing and leant over the banister to see who it was. The fog drifted in through the open door and floated around the hall as a man in a black overcoat stepped inside. He took off his hat and handed it to Mel.

In his other hand he had a doctor's bag.

'Alice,' called William. 'There's an exorcist here to see you.'

'What's an exorcist?' asked Aaron.

'He makes you puke up bad demons,' I said. 'Wait a minute! I've got it!'

'Got what?' said the others. They looked scared, like they half expected a little red man with a forked beard, sharp horns and a long pointy tail to shoot out of my mouth!

'Got the revenge!' I said. 'I bet you a million pounds that this exorcist is another of William and Mel's scams. So why don't we scam them back!'

Aaron and Ralph nodded. 'How?' said Ralph.

'We're going to need a dead body,' I said.

very concerned

The exorcist was waiting in the hall with a serious face. He took my hand, shuddered like I was repulsive to him and uttered these words. 'Time is short. We must hurry.'

It seemed I was indeed possessed and needed help immediately. Mel sent Aaron and Ralph home telling them that what was about to happen was far too gruesome for human eyes.

'That's what we were hoping,' said Ralph. 'Can't we stay?'

'We won't say a word,' said Aaron.

'No,' said Mel, pushing them out the door and slamming it shut.

We cleared the kitchen table and I lay down.

'I need herbs and a live chicken,' said the exorcist. 'Switch off the lights, close all the windows and nobody touch the kettle. We don't have tea till we're done! Tell me honestly, Alistair, does your head rotate the full three hundred and sixty degrees? Is your vomit green? Does your hair fall

150

into tangles? Do your eyes glow red in a demonic sort of way?'

'No,' I said. 'Never!' I put on a faraway kind of voice as if I was entering a trance, just to get everyone in the mood.

'It will happen,' said the exorcist, 'if I don't give you the full works. Light the herbs!'

'I couldn't find any,' said William. 'I got a bouquet garni instead.'

'I can't light that,' said the exorcist, 'I'll start a fire.' He seemed disappointed. 'Cut the chicken's neck and pour the blood over Alistair's head!'

That's herbs in a bag

William laughed nervously.

'It's a frozen chicken,' he said. 'No blood.' So they rubbed the frozen giblets in my hair, which was quite uncomfortable actually and made

151

my scalp ache from the cold.

Then the exorcist took some candles from his bag and stuck one to each corner of the table. He took out some chalk and drew a star on the floor.

'Are you scared yet?' asked William. So this was why Mel and William were doing this. To see how far they could go before I cried and begged them to stop.

'Yes,' I said. 'Very scared. Petrified. In fact . . . Oh, William, something's happening to my arm.'

'What is it?' said Mel. 'You're turning blue. Alistair, what are you doing?'

'I think I'm . . .' I stuttered a bit like the words wouldn't come out. I blew bubbles of spit out my mouth. And then I died.

'Alistair?' That was William. 'Alistair!'

'ALISTAIR!' That was Mel. 'What's happened? He's stopped breathing!'*

'YOU'VE KILLED HIM.'

'I haven't killed him,' said the exorcist. 'I haven't touched him.'

'Well, make him better.'

'How can I make him better? I'm a media student.' And he threw off his exorcist wig and stormed out of the front door. I recognized him as one of Mel's A-level mates.

'WHAT ARE WE GOING TO DO?'
she shouted.

Make Amends

'Make amends,' said a ghostly voice through the kitchen window. Mel and William froze in terror as the voice echoed up from the bowels of the earth. 'Repent! Give up your wordly goods!'

Then they both started crying! It was brilliant.

'Put the money from both of your bank accounts – that's *all* your allowance mind you, not half – into Alistair's Post Office account immediately! If you do not, I, Trog the Mighty Ghost of Revenge, will personally do you in. William, be nice to your younger brother from now on. Mel, never put your clothes in his wardrobe again . . .'

Unfortunately Mel and William had twigged us. They pulled open the back door and found Aaron and Ralph under the window, shouting into a tin bucket.

'Ho-ho-ho!' said my big brother and sister. 'Very funny! Most amusing! You can open your eyes now, Alice.' I opened my eyes. 'Did you really expect us to fall for that old joke?'

'Yes,' I said. 'And you did.'

That was when we all heard a loud knock on the inside of the larder door.

'Oh what a wizard wheeze!' mocked

William. 'You've got Mum in on this as well
have you? Planted her in the larder?'

'No,' I said, because I hadn't. Then the
larder door swung open and standing by the
onions was Great Uncle Crawford wearing
only the underpants we buried him in. His
skin was bright blue.

'There you are, young William,' he said, grabbing my speechless brother by the front of his shirt. 'When you took my good suit off to put your little brother's one on me, where did you put it, you eejit? It's freezing cold buried down here without my clothes on!'

As I recall, everyone screamed and ran away!

Except the ghost of Great Uncle Crawford of course. Seeing as he was over from the Old Country he thought he'd make himself useful.

He'd always had a soft spot for Mum.

He ran through the wall into Dad's bedroom and shouted, 'And you can get up and all, you skiving bag of bones!'

Dad shot out of bed so fast he hit his head on the lampshade! I think he might be cured!

Spent day on loo making nervous bum soup.

Dad has gone back to work. Mum is singing. Great Uncle Crawford has got his suit and is back in the ground. Everything is back to normal.

Complimentary copy of in-flight magazine arrived from the men's store at Heathrow Airport. Joy! The photo of me on the front cover is a head and shoulders shot. You can't see below my neck, so I'll never know if my willy was sticking out of the front of my trousers or not! I can once again rejoin the human race with my dignity intact.

Mel finally went out on her date with Andy. Sadly her rich, hotshot lover-boy turned out to be a very ordinary cheapskate.
I can't think why!

Apparently, Andy received an anonymous phone call telling him that Mel was a simple girl who hated glitz and glamour. If he was thinking of taking her to the Ritz he should cancel immediately, because she hated all that lovely food and chandeliers and famous people at the next tables. If he really wanted to impress her he should take her to a Pizza Hut, let her pay for her own meal afterwards, dump her at the bus stop to make her own way home! Don't think we'll be seeing Andy again!

Is that so, Alice? I thought you might be plotting something like this, you little toad? Well, two can play at that game.
Your loving sister
Mel

0/10
This diary is the shoddiest piece of work I have seen for ages. Appalling spelling and flouts every grammatical rule in the book. You have obviously NOT been paying attention in my English lessons. SATURDAY MORNING DETENTIONS TILL THE END OF YOUR SCHOOL LIFE! You have a lovely sister and should be grateful that she brought me your diary. I know I am.

Pigeon

THE WAR DIARIES OF ALISTAIR FURY

Bugs on the Brain

Jamie Rix

BONSAI!
THIS IS
WAR

My big brother and sister, William and Mel, may be older than me and bigger than me, but they're not cleverer than me. Just because the chips of the world are stacked against me like a potato mountain doesn't mean they can beat me. Revenge will be mine!

Or rather mine and the Revengers', and a boa constrictor called Alfred's. Let loose the snakes of doom and see how they like it then! I shall have my revenge before you can say 'peanut butter and jam sandwiches'! Actually I shouldn't have mentioned peanut butter and jam sandwiches. Forget you ever read that. If you don't, I may have to kill you.

The first book in a brilliant and hilarious series by award-winning comic writer, Jamie Rix.